PRAISE FOR MURDER AT BROADCAST PARK

"The writing is sharp, flowing and tight. It reads like a motion picture, except Bill paints the pictures with words instead of a camera. The entire book I felt like I was sitting in a movie theater watching a mystery unfold. It was an effortless enjoyable read. So many books these days are loaded with fluff that you start to lose interest, that was not the case in this story. Bill has a natural sense for editing, which keeps the action moving forward. The story was told in many ways in the spirit of classic radio shows. You have to have an excellent ear to write like this. The story seemed so real at times I found myself asking "did this really happen at a Santa Barbara TV station" It's really hard to believe that this is story is told by a first time author. It's polished writing that obviously comes from years of life experience put to good use. This will not be the last time we hear from Bill, can't wait to see where he takes us on his next writing adventure."

—Jeff Kelly, TV Meterologist

"Having spent the last 20+ years in the broadcast industry, I have been lucky to meet many wonderful and talented people but none more so than the amazing, Bill Evans. Everyone always asks me, what is it like inside a TV station newsroom and Evans gives you a peek behind the cameras with his Murder at Broadcast Park! A true thriller; a "who done it" that you won't be able to put down; and simply put, a must read!"

—Blake Fulton

"Murder, sex scandals and cover-ups. It sounds like a great news day until you find out: you are the news! Murder at Broadcast Park takes you inside a small market TV station as a broadcast management team faces the worst nightmare they could ever imagine. As veteran TV station executive, Bill Evans is uniquely qualified to take you on this thrilling ride in front of and behind the TV news camera. You'll learn what makes the bosses tick and see what happens when someone makes them sweat."

—Dana Beards, Political Reporter, Capitol Television News Service

"A serious page-turner for serious 'who done it' fans. Don't read the first page of Murder at Broadcast Park unless you plan to race through every page until the end. Vivid and memorable characters. A twisty plot that keeps you guessing. And all of it in laid back Santa Barbara where murders are not the norm. Right? In his sojourn novel Bill Evans proves himself to be a master story teller. I can't wait for his next one. Hint. Hint."

—David Welch, Talk Show Host, WRNR

"I was hooked on the first page and then could not put this book down. Murder at Broadcast House captured me with real characters and a great story. A perfect escape book until I realized how realistic it really was."

—Jim Doyle, Founder, Jim Doyle & Associates

"Bill Evans possesses an incredible broadcasting and marketing mind. But until penning Murder At Broadcast Park, Bill's equally incredible mystery writer mind was a well-kept secret. He keeps readers' guessing with expert misdirection; cleverly weaving the storyline through one surprise after another. Add Murder At Broadcast Park to your must read book list - immediately!"

—John Hannon, President, Jim Doyle & Associates, author of the Amazon best-selling book series, *Engaged Management*

"A great murder mystery wrapped in a terrific primer about how local TV works! Page turning fun, with strong characters and great dialogue!"

—Patrick Evans, CBS Local 2 Chief Meteorologist, Host, Eye on the Desert

"Lights..camera..Homicide ..Broadcasting Icon Bill Evans has crafted a tantilizing tale.. a real sex, lies and videotape odyssey into a dark side of the TV news business Sordid..salacious..from beginning to end."

—Phil Blauer, News Anchor, FOX 5, San Diego

"Bill Evans has created a fabulous look "inside a working Newsroom" while at the same time, crafting a "page turning" thriller that will have you glued to every scene. As someone who spent 54 years in Newsrooms from New York, Los Angeles, and Dallas, to Reno, Idaho Falls, and Bozeman, I LOVED IT!"

—Ted Dawson, Former Sportscaster KABC-Los Angeles

Murder At Broadcast Park
by Bill Evans

ISBN 978-1-63393-491-7

Published by

köehlerbooks™

210 60th Street
Virginia Beach, VA 23451
800-435-4811
www.koehlerbooks.com

by

BILL EVANS

I

THE ASSIGNMENT DESK is exactly what it sounds like. It's the heart of the newsroom, the pulsating epicenter of a local TV news station. Which is why John couldn't quite figure out why he was running it. He was fresh out of college, practically an inexperienced kid. Not only was he deciding the local news stories of the day, but he also determined the level of importance they held. Nonetheless, here he was, controlling news coverage for a network affiliate in Santa Barbara, a job that would be the stepping stone he needed to become the reporter he wanted so badly to be. Hell, everyone knows in the business you take the job that's offered to you, no questions asked. That's how you break into the TV news business.

John usually was among the first to arrive. Reporters and other staffers would trickle in a bit later, waiting for assignments, checking emails, and drinking coffee. Looking up from his desk, John realized that almost everyone that made up the morning news crews was present.

Part of John's route was to turn on the studio lights to warm the room and prepare the set for the morning newscast. The room was typically dark and sometimes drafty from high ceilings.

Just as John flipped on the lights he saw something at the anchor desk—something very odd. He moved closer.

* * *

Barry Burke was used to the phone ringing at all hours of the night. He expected it, even, since he was the news director of the Santa Barbara CBS affiliate. His experiences in this market and several others taught him that when someone from work calls in the middle of the night the story was usually big. But the call from John, the young assignment desk editor, was even bigger than he could have imagined.

"What?" Barry yelled into the phone when John disclosed what he had found. "What the fuck are you talking about? What do you mean you found Steve Johnson dead? Have you called 911? Did you try CPR? Talk to me son. What's going on there?"

Barry's voice was gruff from a lifetime of smoking. His hands shook as he plucked a Marlboro from the pack by his nightstand. He'd be smoking a lot over the next few days. Steve Johnson was a popular morning anchor and had been for a dozen years. News of his death would rock the community.

John had taken a deep breath to calm his nerves and his voice as he further explained what he discovered.

"When I got to the station a few minutes ago, I found Steve sitting at the news desk with a rope around his neck. His lips were blue and his eyes were shut, but his mouth was open, his tongue was hanging out, and it was puffy. I . . . I tried to take the rope off him and put him on the ground to see if there was a pulse. I don't know what to do."

"Okay, okay. Calm down. I want you to hang up the phone and call 911. Now. Then start calling the morning team to get on standby. I want everyone present. Don't tell them anything. I'm on my way. I'll be there in five." With that, Barry hung the phone up. Like a fireman getting dressed for a four-alarm fire, Barry was up and almost out the door when the female voice caught him off guard. He had completely forgotten about the guest in his bed.

"What's going on, Mr. Burke?" The "Mr. Burke" seemed laughable when you considered everything they'd done that evening, all night long. The news director and his new news intern were way past formalities. But of course, this wasn't anything new for Barry. He'd gone through three wives, the last one being six years ago. He loved the perks from his position, especially the one enticing young women by promising them their "big break" into network TV.

"Go back to sleep. I've got to go into the station," Barry whispered, hoping Tami wouldn't detect the panicky undertone of his voice.

"Anything I can do? You need a reporter to fill in?" Tami was an intern on break from college pining for any on-air experience. She was perfect for Barry. She was only here for a couple of months before she had to return to USC to finish out her journalism degree. There were some things the classroom didn't prepare her for in this line of work. It didn't bother her; she was a natural at getting men to pay attention to her and provide her with what she wanted. It was a trade-off she was willing to make in the interest of her career. Plus, a job would be waiting when she graduated.

"Go back to sleep," Barry repeated as he ran out the door. By the time he got to his car he was already on the phone with his friend, Detective Richard Tracy.

"Richard, this is Barry. You had better get over to the station pronto. Steve Johnson's been found dead. I'll meet you there."

Barry and Tracy had become close over the years. Drinking buddies, even. Tracy was also a product of three divorces. It seemed that being a detective and being a news director had a lot of similarities.

As Barry filled in his detective friend, he asked if they could keep it somewhat quiet until they could figure out what exactly was going on. It's not easy to be a local TV news station and be the top story at the same time.

How do we investigate and break our own story? Barry thought as he dashed to his car. From there, he called his general manager, the station's top executive. The phone rang only once and the voice on the other end was crisp and alert, as if the person on the line had never even slept. That was the perception that Lisa wanted to portray.

She worked hard to get her GM stripes. Coming to the company as news talent, it was hard to be taken seriously. Over the years, Lisa moved from news and worked her way up through sales. Lisa picked sales because she realized that was where the real money was. Quickly, she rose to local sales manager, followed by national sales manager, and ultimately general sales manager. Her quick rise was not unusual due to performance and sharp wit, although the good looks and great personality didn't hurt. In Barry's eyes, she was a star. And when the GM spot opened up four years ago, it was hers for the taking.

"Good morning, Barry. A little early, isn't it?"

"Lisa, we've got a problem. A big problem."

"What's going on?" Lisa's voice was calm, but urgency started to creep into her tone.

"Steve Johnson is dead. The new kid on the assignment desk found him this morning when he opened up the studio," Barry explained.

"What? What do you mean he's dead?" The GM was now wide awake.

"Lisa, he's dead. The police are on their way to the station right now. I don't know anything more. I'll see you as soon as you can get there. I'll be there in three minutes."

Without saying goodbye, Lisa hung up the phone and bolted to get dressed. She woke up her husband to tell him what she could, which wasn't much, and took off for the station. News people are a funny breed. They love drama. They love mystery and thinking they have the next big story of the year. Covering murders and death for a newsroom is routine. Covering one of their own, and also inside their newsroom, would be extraordinary for everyone.

***

Barry pulled into the station parking lot as the first responders were arriving. John's 911 call only said a body had been found in the studio. Nothing else. The morning news team and a few of the top reporters and anchors were all called to come in as soon as possible, and most were already assembled in the newsroom. Details were withheld, but the word of a death had already leaked out to staffers. No one was allowed into the studio. The station's security guard was posted at the door by John.

Then, in a rush, the police arrived, led by Detective Tracy and Barry, the station's news director. The two of them and John went into the studio to surveil the scene. The detective then summoned a couple of his officers to examine the scene.

"John, can we talk?" Tracy asked. He was gray-haired and about the same age as John's boss.

"It's okay John, Detective Tracy is a good cop. You can trust him," Barry said.

John chuckled on the inside at the detective's name. Richard Tracy? Really? He swirled around in his chair, stood, and shook Tracy's hand. He wanted to ask about how cruel his parents must have been to name their son Richard Tracy, but they probably never envisioned their son becoming a detective.

"Can we use that room over there to talk?" the detective asked, pointing to a door off to the side.

"Yes, sir. Let me just get someone to sit at the desk for me," John replied. The assignment desk was the one desk that was never left empty. That was one of the first things John learned in his short career.

John called over Carlos, a reporter, to fill in while he went off with the detective. Both men entered the edit suite, which was barely big enough for the two of them with all of its equipment. The edit suite is where reporters go to "cut" their stories for the newscast. The two men sat at the only chairs in the booth.

"John, you were the first to arrive this morning. Tell me exactly what you saw."

"I usually start my shift around three each morning. That gives me a chance to put things together for our morning show. I walked in the back door and headed down the hall."

"Is this typical? Meaning you do this every morning?" Tracy asked.

"Yes, it's my routine. I do this every morning," John said. "I'm almost always the first person here. So, I go down the hall, stop at the studio doorway, and reach in to turn on the studio lights. This gives the lights a chance to warm up the room a little. The studio is the coldest room in the station. When I hit the light switch this morning I saw someone sitting at the anchor desk. At first, I thought someone was playing a joke on me. But then I noticed something wasn't right."

Tracy could tell John was very nervous describing the scene to him. "What wasn't right?" Tracy asked.

"I don't know. But I had a feeling that something was very wrong." John said.

"Okay, When you saw someone sitting in the anchor chair what did you do?" The detective was prompting John to remember every detail.

"At first, nothing. I just stood in the doorway trying to figure out what was going on and who was there."

John was sweating and felt like he was slurring his words. He could feel his pulse pounding. *Maybe I wouldn't make a good investigative reporter after all,* he thought. "I took a step inside the studio and that's when I recognized him."

"Saw what?" The detective's voice rose an octave.

"I saw Steve. He was sitting in the anchor chair with the rope around his neck as if he hung himself." John was trying to keep his composure.

Steve Johnson was thirty-seven years old and had been at the station for eleven years. He was the number one anchor/newsman in the area and very well respected by everyone. Steve had a wife and three kids. He was not confrontational and always punctual. He never missed a day, and he always delivered the news. His demise would be huge news.

"As I made out what I was seeing, I ran over to Steve. But I could tell that he was already dead," John said.

"Your first call at that point went to?" The detective didn't say what he already knew. He wanted the kid to tell him.

"Barry Burke. Barry is the news director and my boss. I didn't know who else to call," John stated.

"Nine-one-one would have been my first call," said the detective, not hiding his irritation in the slightest.

"Maybe it's the news person in me or just my lack of experience. I don't really know. I called the first person I could think of, and that was Barry." John was obviously getting upset at Tracy's apparent jab.

"What did Mr. Burke say to you on the phone?" Detective Tracy asked.

"He told me to call 911 and then start calling news people in. The morning news team hadn't arrived yet, and Barry wanted that team in as soon as possible. He also asked me not to tell anyone anything. He said he would be in as soon as he could get dressed and make the drive."

Barry only lived seven minutes from the station. He arrived with the first police cars now parked with lights flashing in the station parking lot.

"Did you touch the body?" the detective asked.

"I got Steve off the chair and laid him down on the floor. I tried to get the rope off his neck, but all I could do was loosen it. That's when I threw up next to his body." John started shaking as he described the scene to the detective.

"Tell me what you think happened to Steve." Detective Tracy wanted to see if this young kid had any ideas as to what happened.

"I don't have any idea. I'm the new guy here. I've only been here four months," John said, trying to explain his answer.

"You think he killed himself? You think someone murdered him? Anyone at the station hate this guy? You ever hear anyone threaten Steve Johnson?" Tracy was trying to get anything he could by firing off question after question.

John's head was spinning now. He hadn't given any thought to who might have done this, why, or even if Steve had killed himself. But for a moment, John wondered what could have been so bad for this anchor that he would have committed suicide.

"I have no clue as to what happened," John muttered as the noise in the newsroom started to pick up. Employees started pouring in. The horror of the newsroom being a murder scene was oddly a source of excitement for this news station. There is nothing more thrilling for a newsroom than a catastrophe. Even if one of their own is involved.

2

TODD AND JAKE arrived in separate cars, but at the same time. They tried to keep their relationship a secret, but newsrooms are small and everyone knows everyone's business. Despite their discretion, everyone knew they were in a relationship.

Todd was a morning reporter out in the field, while Jake co-anchored the morning news behind the comfort of his news desk. Both had come into the station under different circumstances, but it wasn't long before they discovered they shared the same secret. They became "roommates" to their outside circle, and according to them, everyone was on the outside.

Barry Burke started gathering the news team together in the parking lot to fill them in on what John had found this morning. There was discussion about what—if anything—about Steve Johnson's death the station should report on its morning news. What if their competitors found out what happened and wanted to come over to start reporting on one of their own? The morning news would go on the air at five. They had a little over an hour to put everything together.

Lisa got with Barry as soon as she arrived at the station. "Has anyone called Steve's wife?" asked the GM.

"I think she's out of town," Barry answered.

"Barry, what do I need to know about Steve Johnson before we get too far into this?" Lisa had enough experience with news talent and their extracurricular activities to ask that question. There were rumors about the station's anchor and how he might have had affairs, a lot of them. She thought she better know everything up front so she could do damage control for the station and the station's owner.

"Lisa, all I know is that Steve was found dead this morning. I try not to know too much of what goes on outside of the station with our people." Barry was beginning to think about his own transgressions with interns. Newsrooms had their own casting couch and the news director always owned the couch. No one talked about it, especially if you wanted to continue to work in the business.

The conversation stopped when Detective Tracy and his partner, Skip Reynolds, walked up. Lisa knew both men. That's how it was in a small town when you were the number one news station and had been since the first time you went on air in 1965.

"Detectives, Barry was just filling me in. You got anything you can tell me?"

"Too early to say. We're going to need to talk to everyone, though. Can we set up in your conference room? Lisa, is there anything you can tell us? Anyone have a problem with Steve? Any threatening mail or emails from anyone? Stalkers? Right now we don't have squat." Detective Tracy let his partner do all the talking. He wanted to reserve himself for his buddy Barry.

"Are you saying he didn't hang himself?" Lisa asked.

Detective Reynolds paused. "The coroner will have to tell us. I'm not sure he even died by hanging at this point."

"I thought there was a rope around his neck," the GM said.

"You're right, there was. He was also sitting in his anchor chair, according to the kid's story. How do you hang yourself if you're sitting down? I'm not sure the rope had anything to do with his death. What about his family? Can you tell us anything that might help?" Reynolds asked.

"Well Barry was just saying that his wife might be out of town. I need to call her." She turned from the detectives to face her news director. "Barry, see if you can get me a number?" Barry nodded and walked toward his office with Detective Tracy following.

"Look, Richard. Steve has always been a bit of a player on the side, but I don't want to speculate on anything at this point. Let's just say he wasn't exactly shy around women in the past. But I thought he cleaned up his act and was working on his marriage, trying to make things work. I'm shocked. I don't really know what to say right now."

"We're going to try and reach out to Steve's wife. If you happen to talk to her before we do, let her know that we need to talk to her. For right now we need to start talking to everyone about what they may know or think they know," Detective Tracy said to his friend.

* * *

The control room buzzed as it usually did every morning. "Roll the open. Standby to cue anchors. Cue anchors." The words were spoken in a very controlled but strong voice from the twenty-six-year old director, Tom Bryson. Tom might have sounded in control, but there was no doubt that everyone was on edge this morning. The studio was a crime scene, so delivering the news needed to get done in a makeshift studio from the patio. Luckily, the weather was cooperating and the patio was a perfect setting looking over the Pacific Ocean.

"Good morning, I'm Jake Thomas," the male anchored opened the news show. "And I'm Anne Swanson. Leading off our newscast this morning, a body was found here in the studio of our station, and the circumstances are currently under investigation. As the investigation is ongoing, there is not much we can say at this time. However, as we gather more information, we will be breaking in live to update you throughout the day. Police are here in the building and believe it happened sometime late last evening or early this morning. At this time, they will not be releasing any further details until next of kin has been notified." Anne Swanson was smooth as the female morning anchor.

And with that, the morning news got under way. The station had to say something because newspapers and other TV stations would undoubtedly be asking for a comment. Barry was lost within his thoughts. *They couldn't not report on what is surely going to be the biggest story of the day. You have to stay true to being "the local news leader." And just because you are now the news doesn't mean you can stay away from it. It means the opposite, right? We need to be ahead of this story at every turn.* Barry's mind whirled as he sat in front of his computer screen, having typed the first story into the morning news teleprompter so the morning anchors could start their show. He wondered whether his boss had made contact with Steve Johnson's widow.

* * *

"Janet, this is Lisa, Lisa Campbell from the station. Sorry to bother you so early in the morning."

Just then the message on the other line continued, "Just kidding. I'm not available right now so please leave a detailed message and I'll return the call as quickly as possible."

Lisa was caught completely off-guard thinking she reached her anchor's wife. *Bullshit. I hate those stupid trick messages,* she thought.

"Janet, this is Lisa at the station. Please call me as soon as possible. We have an emergency and I need to talk to you as soon as possible." She hung up the phone, praying to hear from Janet before Janet and her three kids heard the news about her husband from the police or from a media source uncovering Steve's identity, even though no names were being mentioned at this time in their stories.

Detectives Tracy and Reynolds came down the hall to the GM's office. "Lisa, you have a second?" Reynolds asked.

"Come on in. Anything you can tell me yet?" Lisa asked.

The detectives sat. There wasn't anything to tell at this point. The police department was now investigating and interviewing everyone at the station from the receptionist to the janitor. There were no signs of a struggle. No one knew how he died. Maybe by hanging, maybe not.

Reynolds looked over to Lisa. "Were you able to reach Steve's wife?"

"I left her a message on her cell phone. She hasn't called back yet. Maybe you should send a car over to their house and see if anyone's home," Lisa suggested.

"I thought she was out of town?" Reynolds said.

"That's what someone told us, but you never know. I can send Barry over there with you. He knows the wife pretty well."

Tracy jumped at the opportunity to get out of the station for a few minutes so he could smoke. He also knew his friend Barry would appreciate a smoke break. "Why don't I take Barry and go over to the house to see if anyone's home?"

Everyone nodded in agreement. And off the detective went to find the news director.

The drive was two cigarettes and twelve minutes into a quiet neighborhood. The streets were littered with bikes, tricycles, and skateboards, and it was obvious a lot of kids lived on the block. The Johnsons' daughters were ages six, eight, and eleven.

The conversation on the way over was off the record and pure speculation as to what the two friends thought might have happened to the anchorman. The two bantered back and forth asking all the questions they wanted answered. *Did he hang himself? Or was the crime scene staged to look like he did? Why in the studio? Was someone else involved at the station? What's with the chair? What the hell was going on?* A lot of questions with very few answers, but this whole scenario was only hours old.

"Let's knock on the door and see if she's home," the detective said in a very police-like manner.

Barry gave the door a polite three knocks. With no sounds coming from the inside, he knocked louder and not so polite, just in case Steve's wife was in the back of the house. Reynolds noticed the doorbell and pushed it twice while Barry continued to knock.

Still, there were no sounds coming from inside the house. Reynolds suggested they go around back to see if they could see anything inside the house. Something wasn't feeling right for the detective.

It was a typical residential track house with four bedrooms built in early 2000 along with the fifty-four other homes in the neighborhood. Most of the houses had cheap wood fences around the yards. The back gate had a simple latch—easily accessible to anyone who tried. There was one of those four-and-half-foot plastic pools in the backyard as well as a nicer hot tub on the patio off the master bedroom. The windows were all closed and covered with blinds, so the two men couldn't see in. At first glance it appeared no one was home.

Detective Tracy tried the back door, which opened. This caused some tension for the two. They cautiously entered. The detective signaled with his hand for Barry to be quiet. Barry loved this sudden rush of adrenaline. It reminded him of when he would uncover a big story working as a reporter on the streets of Los Angeles.

Before entering the home, Detective Tracy drew his revolver. There didn't seem to be anyone home. The house was silent. Not just quiet. It was silent. Making their way down the hall, the kids' rooms were the first they cleared. The beds were made and rooms were picked up with no signs of the girls. Tracy seemed to relax a little and put his revolver back into his belt-strapped holster. Approaching the master bedroom, the door was open about three quarters. Barry was first to the door and lightly pushed the door open the rest of the way.

Someone was asleep in the bed, presumably Janet. Detective Tracy called out Janet's name as he carefully approached the bed trying not to scare her. Janet didn't respond. This time he was louder as he reached down to touch the back of her shoulder. Janet didn't move and Richard knew by the little touch that she was dead. "Barry, we've got a problem here."

"Let me check to see if she's breathing," Tracy murmured as he tried to get a pulse as well. But Janet was dead and probably had been dead for several hours, he speculated.

"What the fuck?" Barry couldn't believe what was happening. First his news anchor was found dead in the studio and now the anchor's wife is dead in their bed.

"Richard, what was going on here?"

"Not sure, but I need to call this in and get the crime unit out here. Look around and see if you can find the girls anywhere. Maybe they're hiding somewhere in the house, but be careful not to move anything for the crime boys," cautioned the detective.

Barry's news instincts kicked in, and before he started looking around for the girls, he called Lisa, his boss.

"Lisa, it's Barry, we found Janet. She's dead. We found her in their bed."

Lisa's voice was cracking again. "Oh my god, Barry. What is going on here? What about the kids? Are the kids anywhere to be found?"

"The kids don't appear to be here. There are no signs of a struggle and no signs of anything out of the ordinary, but the kids are gone, and Janet is dead."

While Barry talked to Lisa, Detective Tracy was on the phone with his chief of detectives. He needed the CSI team to the house with a coroner. The problem was that most of the crime team was at the station with the only coroner in the county. Steve Johnson's body was still on the studio floor.

"Look Lisa, I know this has everyone spooked right now, but I think we need to be on the air with this story. We need to own this story. We can't let our competitors get ahead of us on a story that is happening in our own building. That would look like we weren't covering the story because it's happening to us."

"Barry? This isn't about covering a news story. We lost a member of our station family, and now his wife. Good god, have some compassion," Lisa countered.

Barry wasn't surprised by his boss's reaction. He had seen this attitude from previous general managers. What he wanted was to scream into his phone. *You can't think like that or you will miss out on the biggest story of the year. You shouldn't give a shit about compassion right now.* That's what he wanted to tell his GM, but he didn't. In Los Angeles and New York, the bigger markets, they understood Barry's hard news attitude and they could care less about compassion. He wasn't sure that attitude would play well in a little market like Santa Barbara. But Barry knew he was right about this one. *Why let anyone get ahead of you on a story that is happening to you?* He pressed Lisa.

"Look, we need to do something. If nothing else we need to put out the information we know right now. It's not going to be long before every news organization in town is on this and that includes the networks from Los Angeles." Being only two hours away, and under the circumstances, this was a story worth covering for the LA stations.

"It's your call, Barry. I brought you here to keep us the number one news station. But you better be careful and sensitive with what you do." And with that Lisa hung up the phone.

Immediately, Barry dialed the assignment desk to speak to the newsroom. He wanted a live truck and a reporter to the house ASAP.

"John, I need you to call everyone in. Get the whole news team to the station as quickly as possible. Now let me speak to Jake." Barry wanted to talk to his morning co-anchor, the person who had the most experience in the newsroom at this time of the morning.

"This is Jake."

"Jake, this is Barry. I need you to send Todd out here with the live truck. I'm at Steve Johnson's house. Get the address off the news roster on my desk. You and Anne need to be ready to do some cut-ins. We found Steve's wife dead in bed. Get moving on this and keep it quiet. I don't want to tip off any of the other stations."

"Got it. I'll get them out the door right away. We'll get ready to do some cut-ins. What about the network? Do you want us pre-empting their morning show?" Jake asked a good question.

"I'll call Tom and work out the cut-ins with him. Tell him I'm going to call him and to have the morning crew ready to go back to work." Barry couldn't help but feel good and excited about breaking this story, even though it involved people he knew very well. Relationships never mattered to the news director. That's what made him a good at his job—and why he had three ex-wives.

Just as his call with Jake ended, his cell phone rang. It was Lisa, his boss.

"Barry, look, I'm nervous about us doing this story prematurely. It's your call, but you better get it right. All eyes are going to be on our station and everyone is going to be watching when this news gets out. Make sure you handle it correctly." She hung up.

Barry found Tracy still in the master bedroom and hanging up from his call with the police chief. "Richard, what can I have my people report? We now have two suspicious deaths. I'm going to break this story as fast as my people can get here and get set up. You gotta give me something."

Tracy was taken back by Barry's attitude. It didn't seem as though he was concerned anymore about these people. It was if they were strangers. Now it was about getting the story out first. "Barry, you gotta be careful here. We have two bodies. We don't know if they've been murdered. Maybe this is a murder-suicide. Maybe it's a double suicide. We don't have any evidence of foul play. We don't have anything but two dead bodies. We've got nothing to say." The detective was giving his friend a reminder to proceed with caution.

Barry was lighting a cigarette. He didn't care that he was still standing in the Johnson house. He passed one across to Tracy and without any hesitation the detective took it. They walked outside and both took long drags. The inhale seemed to relax them a little, if that was possible.

"Look, Barry, I know you want this story, but be careful with how fast you run with this. Right now all we know is that Steve and Janet Johnson are dead. We have to find the kids. What if this is a double murder and the kids have been kidnapped? We don't know, and we can't jeopardize the investigation."

The news director's head was spinning. At that moment he heard the live truck pull up. He could tell because the sound of the brakes the live truck made every time it stopped. He had wanted the chief engineer to get those fixed for the past two months, but it still hadn't been done.

"Barry, they can't park in the driveway. In fact, they need to be across the street. We're going to have to set up a perimeter blocking off the yard and the house. This is an official crime scene now and we need to treat it as such. I've got some gloves for you to wear. Put them on." Tracy held out the gloves.

Barry nodded, taking the gloves from Tracy as he headed outside to have his people move the live truck. He wasn't about to piss off his police buddies. He had worked too long and hard to build these relationships. As Tim, the live truck driver and photographer on this story, moved the truck, Barry talked to Todd. "This is what we have. Steve Johnson was found dead at the station this morning when our morning crew arrived. He had a rope around his neck but was seated in the anchor chair on the news set. A few minutes ago Detective Tracy and I found Steve's wife. She was in bed and dead. We don't know what caused the deaths of either of the victims."

Todd interrupted his news director. "I thought you said Steve had a rope around his neck?"

"He did have a rope around his neck, but it doesn't appear that he was hung or choked. We don't know if it is one murder or two murders or a murder-slash-suicide or a double suicide. Hell, it might be two people who died of natural causes. The point is we don't know."

Todd was taking notes as fast as he could while listening to his frantic news director rehearse talking points. It was interesting to the reporter that Barry had gone from talking about an employee to now talking in terms of "victims." The reporter kept thinking, *Stay cool. This could be the story of a lifetime. This could be my break.*

Every reporter thought that on any big story. They always believed it would be the story to launch their career and land them some national network time where they would be seen and discovered. No one ever tried to burst their bubbles by telling them that rarely, if ever, does that happen. The reporters who worried about the "next big, breaking story" never seemed to go anywhere. The reporters who did a strong, consistent job on every story all the time were the ones landing in the bigger markets. Todd was good, and this story, if he handled it right, would certainly look good on his resume reel.

Barry took a call from Tom Bryson, the director. They were ready to go live as soon as the live truck was operating. The plan was to break into the CBS Morning Show. You never break into a network news program, but this was different. The news directors figured that local stories of this magnitude took precedence over anything else.

Todd had his IFB earpiece in place so he could hear the director count him down. "Three, two, one . . ." Todd stood on the sidewalk in front of the Johnson house, listening to the morning anchor and his partner, Jake Thomas, talking on the air and setting up the live shot everyone was going to see in only seconds.

"Jake, I can tell you right behind me, police are investigating the scene where a second body has been discovered this morning. Steve Johnson, our main news anchor, was found dead in our studio very early this morning and now we are in front of his home where only minutes ago the police discovered Janet Johnson dead inside. We don't have any details as to what caused her death or how it ties into Steve Johnson's death earlier this morning. Police are only beginning their investigation, and we've actually beat their investigators to the scene." Todd thought it was a nice touch to point that fact out so the promotional people could use it in a sound bite. "We'll be here all day and will keep you updated as we get more details in what appears to be a double homicide. I'm Todd Evans for your local news leader CBS 2."

Within seconds of getting off camera Barry was in Todd's face. "Why did you say double homicide? We don't know what this is yet. This is exactly what I covered with you minutes ago. What if it's not a double homicide? Shit. This is the kind of mistake we don't need."

Back at the station the general manager was trying to calm the panicked employees. Her cell phone rang, and not with a number she knew. "This is Lisa."

"Lisa, this is Janet Johnson. You left me a message to call you as soon as I could and I just got your message. Is everything alright?" Lisa was shocked. Her TV station had just reported that Janet was dead.

"Janet, can I ask you where you are? And are the kids with you?" Her voice was so serious that it was haunting to Janet.

"Lisa, what's this about? Has something happened to Steve? What's going on?" Janet wanted answers.

Lisa stayed quiet a few moments as she tried to gather her thoughts. She had to tell Steve's wife about his death, but what did she say about the woman found in her bed?

3

"BARRY, WHO IS THE woman you found dead in the house?" Lisa's question stunned her news director.

"What do you mean, who is the woman? It's Janet Johnson, Steve's wife."

"No, Barry, it's not. I know this because Janet just returned the call I made to her this morning. She has the three kids and they're in Oregon visiting relatives." Lisa's voice took on a stern sound that Barry hadn't heard from his boss ever before. "I told you that if you did something on this story to make sure you played it conservatively and to especially get it right. You've fucked this up. Badly! Not only did your reporter call this a double murder, you reported names of the victims before next of kin were notified, and better still you announced that Janet Johnson was one of the bodies and she's not." Lisa's tone got angrier and heavier with each word.

Barry knew he was in deep shit. He had never heard his boss curse. No one had to tell him how bad this looked. He knew the priority for any news story was accuracy—not who got it first. Who cared if the story was first if it was wrong?

The police crime team arrived at the house. No one had done anything with the body. The woman in the bedroom sure looked like Janet, Barry thought. How could he have gotten this wrong? And if the body wasn't Janet, then who was it, and what was she doing in Steve's bed? Barry couldn't take it out on his reporter because he was the one who identified the body as Steve's wife.

Barry went back inside the house to tell Detective Reynolds about Lisa's phone call. "Do you know if Lisa told Janet about the woman's body in their bed?" Detective Tracy asked.

"I don't have any idea, Richard. I'm not sure what Lisa told her or didn't tell her. I was so rattled once she told me she talked to Janet that I didn't grasp too much more of the conversation."

"Call her back and find out what she told her. We're going to want to talk to Steve's wife as soon as possible. Find out if Lisa knows when she'll be back in town."

Barry was still rattled, far more than he could remember. It was like this scene was playing out in his head and he wasn't really a part of it.

"Lisa, it's Barry. Detective Tracy wanted me to find out what you shared with Mrs. Johnson. Did you tell her about the woman we found in her bed?"

"I didn't share anything with her except that Steve was found dead this morning at the station," his boss replied.

"The police want to talk to her as soon as possible," Barry said.

"She should be here late this afternoon. She was going to jump on the next plane she could get out on," Lisa explained.

"Let's hope she doesn't hear anything on the radio or TV about the other woman," Barry reiterated.

"Any idea as to who she is?" Lisa wanted answers so she knew what kind of damage control she had to do to protect the station. That reminded her that she had to call Stewart Simpson, the owner of her Santa Barbara station. Lisa never liked Stewart hearing news from anyone but her—especially bad news. "Barry, I have to go call Stewart. Keep me informed as soon as you have more information. In fact, you should get back to the station so you can run your troops from here." Lisa hung up.

Barry shook his head, hoping none of his competitors repeated his station's on-air gaffe.

***

"Stewart, Lisa here. We've had a pretty dramatic morning and I need to fill you in."

"You mean about Steve Johnson found dead on the news set and his wife found dead at home?" Stewart said with an indignant tone.

"How'd you know that?" Lisa asked.

"I got calls of condolences from people I know in Santa Barbara who saw it on our station. So, what's your game plan? Do the police have any theories or suspects? Any idea as to what this is about?" The owner asked.

"Right now we don't know anything and there seems to be a lot more to this story that we need to find out about," Lisa said. "But, Stewart, there's been a mistake in our reporting. Mrs. Johnson is alive and vacationing in Oregon with her three kids.

"You mean the woman found in Steve's bed isn't Steve's wife?"

"Yes, that is exactly what I am saying."

"So we reported that the wife of our anchor may have been murdered, but she's actually alive. Christ almighty," Stewart barked. "I'm flying in later today. Let's meet at my place around seven. You can fill me in then," Stewart said.

By the time Lisa hung up the phone the station was filling up with employees. The station had ninety-seven employees and everyone arrived by nine, including anyone who was not scheduled to work. Lisa hit the intercom button to Sandy's desk outside her executive office. "Sandy, let everyone know we will meet in the newsroom for a staff meeting in fifteen minutes."

Lisa hoped to dispel rumors and discuss a game plan for dealing with this situation today and the days ahead.

Barry walked passed Sandy as she was hanging up with their boss. As he knocked on the door he opened it and walked in. Lisa was used to the news director walking into her office unannounced. And formalities were not important right now. "Barry, you have anything new from the house?"

"Lisa, the crime lab is there and going over every detail. It didn't appear there were any signs of a struggle. Honestly, I thought the woman I saw lying down in that bed was Janet. I don't know how I missed that it wasn't her."

"That's a normal assumption for anyone to make. The problem is that you're a goddamn newsman. You're supposed to get it right. And what about stories coming from any of our competitors? Are they doing anything on this yet?"

"Once we did our live shot the idiots over at ABC showed up at the house and they have another crew in our parking lot right now. NBC still hasn't a clue, but they'll eventually show up."

Barry knew he would be hearing about this screw-up for a long time.

***

Detective Reynolds continued interviewing everyone at the television station who he thought might be able to provide leads. The coroner had begun to remove the body from the studio to take it back to his lab. A full autopsy would be performed to determine a cause of death. The body at the house would be arriving at the lab too after the coroner perused the crime scene.

"Richard, what do you got?" Reynolds took the call from his fellow detective. "A dead body, and not much else. No signs of a struggle. No outward cause of death that we can see. No identification, but this girl looks familiar. I'm going to send you a couple of pictures on your cell phone. Maybe someone at the station can identify her. What do you have over there?" Reynolds asked his fellow detective.

"The coroner just left and is heading over to the house. His assistants are taking Steve's body to the lab. Janet Johnson will be back in town later this afternoon. I told her we'd have her plane met and have her brought to the police station to meet with us. That way the press won't get to her first. Send me the picture of the dead woman and I'll show it around to see if anyone knows her."

Tracy used his cell phone camera to send the pictures. While waiting for the pictures to come into focus he went and found Barry walking out of Lisa's office. He knew Barry could help him download the picture and probably even print it out so they could show it around. This woman sure looked like Janet Johnson, at least lying face down. The picture took a little time to come in clear on the little cell phone screen.

"Shit. Shit, shit, shit," exclaimed Barry. "How can this be?" His words attracted Reynolds' attention and drew the attention of Lisa standing in her office. The two turned and walked into the GM's office and closed the door behind them.

"Lisa, look at this picture of the dead woman at Steve's house. Do you recognize her?" Barry asked.

"Should I? Who is she?" Lisa asked.

"She's a paid intern that started a few weeks ago in the newsroom. Steve told me he was mentoring her on her reporting skills. Fuck. What a mess we got here."

"So she's an employee? Jesus, do you know how much trouble this can cause us? Where is the girl's family? What's her name?" Lisa was starting to wonder what curse the station was under.

"Jesse Anderson. She came here from Texas on a paid internship. I think her family is all in Texas," Barry said.

"You better get me their contact information so I can notify them before the medical examiner does. You also better let the police know who she is. We don't want to be concealing anything. We need to be transparent in our news coverage and everything we are doing. I mean that, Barry. Do not fuck with me on this. You've already fucked the story up and the station pretty bad."

Barry knew this would be the theme for a while and he'd just have to listen and take it.

"Lisa, we better go to the newsroom for the staff meeting. You need to tell people what's going on and whatever else you can share with them." Barry touched her arm. "We'll get through this. I'll take care of the on-air stuff. You handle the staff."

The newsroom was barely big enough for more than fifty employees in the news department. Rarely had the entire news contingent been there at the same time. The department worked in shifts throughout the day, like factory workers. A few worked overnight, and most of the time reporters, producers, and cameramen were out of the building covering news. Now the room held almost everyone. The mood was somber.

Lisa stepped in front of the staff at the front of the room. "Everyone, can I have your attention please? First off, I appreciate you coming in today for those who were scheduled off. As you probably know, Steve Johnson was found dead this morning on the news set. Our hearts and prayers go out to Steve's family. What you might not know is that Jesse Anderson, who only joined our team three weeks ago, was found dead this morning as well, at the Johnsons' home." Lisa purposely left out the fact that she was found in Steve's bed and that Steve's wife wasn't home. "The detectives would like me to ask anyone with any information at all to please let them know. You can let me know, or Barry, if that is easier. We need any and all information you have that might help the police solve this case. Do not try to censor any information. If you think it might be relevant, then you need to speak up. And let me reiterate that this is a personnel matter *inside* the station. So the less you say the better." She turned to her news director. "Barry, you want to run down with everyone what you need from the news department?"

"Thanks, Lisa," Barry said, and with that he launched into his game plan for all-day coverage featuring cut-ins, live shots, and newscasts. Lisa ducked out of the meeting to go back to her office to call Jesse's parents. Two of these calls in one day could take it out of you, and Lisa was feeling the pain.

The phone rang twice before a man answered. "Vic Anderson, how can I help you?" The voice was deep and very strong.

"Mr. Anderson, this is Lisa Campbell, the general manager at CBS 2 in Santa Barbara. I have some bad news to report to you." Lisa was trying to keep her voice calm.

Mr. Anderson was very quiet. His daughter was a handful growing up and always pushed her boundaries. She was very beautiful and on the fast track to whatever it was she was working on. Her parents didn't want to know what they already thought she was into. They knew she was in trouble when they found out she had an affair with the professor of her broadcast ethics class. For the ex-military father, it was hard to accept that his daughter was not only promiscuous but used her sex appeal to get ahead in her career. This call, although heartbreaking for him, was not totally shocking. That wasn't lost on Lisa as she explained what they knew so far.

When she finished, Mr. Anderson simply said, "Thank you for calling," and hung up the phone.

While Lisa was calling the Andersons, the two detectives now working the case were at Jesse Anderson's condo. Tracy and Detective Reynolds were surprised at how nice it was and what a good area it was in. She certainly didn't make that kind of money as a paid intern. The relationship between Tracy and

Barry provided some insight for the detective as to what people made in television in this market. Santa Barbara media didn't have any problems attracting people to work there because it was in a "sunshine market." People traded high wages to live in a nice place. Jesse was a paid intern, meaning she made less then what a regular employee would make. And that wasn't much. She did receive college credits for the internship.

Jesse's two-bedroom condo was extremely neat. Nothing seemed out of place. They could tell by the contents in her closet that she lived alone. It appeared to the two men that this girl who should barely be making it lived above her pay level. She might be living above their salary level.

"Maybe her family has money," Tracy said as the two continued to look around. It felt strange to both as they noticed there were no family pictures anywhere. It looked like a decorated model home. That seemed very odd.

"Maybe she was a hooker on the side. That would explain the different style of clothes hanging in each bedroom closet," Reynolds speculated. In the master bedroom hung what would appear normal, everyday clothes that she probably went to work in at the station. In the second closet there were very high-end designer clothes and shoes.

The reason the detectives knew she lived by herself was because the second bedroom didn't have a bed in it, just a fold-out couch. Both men made a note that they would want to seize the computer. Nothing else was out of place. Where did her money come from?

* * *

The NBC and ABC stations had gotten on the story and it was leading their noon newscasts. CBS 2 didn't have a noon newscast. Barry didn't think it was worth staffing for because the noon audience was small. Most people were at work or lunch. Barry's station was already number one in the market anyway by putting resources into the early morning and evening newscasts.

Barry decided the best way to stay ahead of everyone on this story—their story—was with a cut-in every thirty minutes. They would string out the information and not give everything away in one or two reports. There still wasn't much to cover, but Barry knew he'd get the information first because the story was about his people. His dead anchor and dead intern. What else would this story be about? Possibly an affair, but what else? What was Jesse doing in Steve's bed? Why was Steve dead in his anchor chair with a rope around his neck while Jesse, a beautiful twenty-something, was in his bed? How did you explain that, especially since Steve worked the eleven o'clock newscast the night before? That meant he would have gotten home at the earliest around midnight. John found him in the chair just before 3 a.m. and he was already dead. What happened in those three hours?

Barry wasn't the only one who had put together this time frame. After visiting the dead girl's condo, Tracy and Reynolds were running down the same time line with their police chief. They had more unanswered questions than answers.

By the afternoon, news blogs and websites would light up about the morning activities. Speculation was flying, and nothing was close to the truth. One person would write that Jesse had secretly married Steve weeks ago when she arrived at CBS 2 after Steve had secretly divorced his wife. Another wrote that Jesse was an adopted daughter and sex slave to both Steve and his wife, Janet. It was like news people wanted to make up their own headlines and forget about any hurt these accusations and lies might cause family or true friends of the deceased. It wasn't only the competition writing vicious rumors. These blogs were fun for coworkers, especially jealous coworkers. That was the news business.

Barry told his detective friends about the blogs and websites, and the police decided to assign someone to monitor and trace all the writings. Maybe the real killer would post something, or maybe a lead would be generated by all this activity on the internet. In the same phone call, Barry was asked something he wasn't prepared for.

"Barry, how much were you paying Jesse Anderson?"

"She was a paid intern. I don't think she made more than eight or nine dollars an hour and she wasn't even working thirty hours a week. Why?" the news director asked.

"Do you know if she had a second income?" his detective friend asked.

"I don't know, but I don't think so. She seemed to spend all her extra time here working and learning her craft even when she wasn't on the clock. She could do that because she was an intern. What's this about?" Barry asked.

"Have you seen where she lives? It's in the nice part of town where she has a two-bedroom condo. She has expensive designer clothes and nice furniture. Do you know if her family has money?"

"I really don't know anything about her." Barry was thinking this was the first break in the case. Maybe Jesse had a double life. The two friends ended the call but Barry was starting to think there was a lot more to this than he even first imagined.

Todd knocked on Barry's door and was waved into the room. Todd, without asking, closed the door behind him.

"Barry, I just want you to know that I'm here to do whatever you need me to do. I can anchor the newscasts tonight if you want. Then I'll come back in the morning and anchor my morning show. Whatever you need. I just wanted you to know."

"Thanks, Todd. I appreciate that. I'll let you know. Go ahead and get back to work."

Barry was surprised it had taken that long before someone was in his office already pitching for Steve's job, the number one anchor position. It wouldn't be the only time this would happen today. In the next four hours Barry would hear from three more of his news people. They all let Barry know that he could count on them, that whatever he needed he just had to ask. And, oh by the way, "I'd be glad to anchor tonight and fill in for Steve, if you'd like."

Barry hated when news people pretended to care. He wished they would just come out and say, "I want Steve's job and I'll do whatever the fuck you need me to do to get it." No pretense. No bullshit. If they would just be honest about it.

***

Barry and Lisa wanted to be at the police station around noon when Janet showed up to talk to the police. They knew that wasn't appropriate. They wanted to be there to find out what Janet knew. Then they would know how deep the station was involved in this double whatever it was. There was still no confirmation that it was a double murder. It might be days before the coroner could tell them anything. At this point the police had nothing to work with and they weren't sure Janet was going to be very helpful.

The detectives greeted Janet at the counter in the lobby of the police station. It was obvious to both detectives that she had been crying, probably most of the day. There was a person with her that no one recognized. He had the look of lawyer written all over him. *Why would Janet need to bring a lawyer to this meeting?* the detectives thought.

"Janet, I'm Detective Tracy. This is Detective Reynolds. We're sorry for your loss. Can we go into the conference room where we can talk?" Tracy was trying to be as comforting as possible in this situation.

"Gentlemen, I'm Byron Culpepper, Mrs. Johnson's attorney." Now the conversation took on a different tone.

"Mr. Culpepper, why does Mrs. Johnson need an attorney?" questioned Detective Tracy.

"I'm a family friend and the family thought I should accompany her to the station to talk with you. As you can imagine, this has been very stressful news for her and she isn't holding up very well, but she wanted to cooperate with you as quickly as possible," the attorney said.

"By all means, please join us." The four walked down the hallway to the conference room. This was not an interrogation room, but simply a conference room used for meetings.

"Can I offer you something to drink, Mrs. Johnson? Coffee or a Coke? Some water maybe?" Detective Reynolds offered.

"Coffee would be great." The answer came from the attorney, which annoyed the detectives.

"For you, Mrs. Johnson? Anything?" Detective Reynolds asked again.

She didn't say anything and barely raised her head, only to shake it no. She lifted her eyes in the direction of the other side of the table. "Officers, what can you tell me about my husband? How did he die?"

"Mrs. Johnson, we don't know just yet. He was found very early this morning sitting in his anchor chair on the news set with a rope around his neck. We are still waiting on the coroner's report to tell us how he died," Reynolds explained.

Janet's eyes opened up and fear showed on her face. Not fear from being frightened, but the kind of fear from hearing something scary for the first time. "Did he hang himself?" she asked.

"Janet . . . may we call you Janet?" asked Reynolds. She just nodded. "Janet, we don't know anything at this time. The coroner will perform an autopsy tomorrow to determine the cause of death. It doesn't appear that hanging was the cause, though. Steve was sitting in his chair and not hanging above it. There didn't appear to be any struggle or stab wounds or bullet holes. He was found sitting in his anchor chair. That is all we know right now."

"Can I see him? I want to go to where he is. Can I see him?" Janet began crying, trying not to become hysterical.

"I'm sorry, Mrs. Johnson. You can't see him until after the autopsy. Is there anything at all you can tell us that might help us figure this out? Why were you away with the kids without Steve?" Detective Tracy asked.

Wiping away the constant, slow flow of tears, she said, "The kids and I went up to see my parents in Bend, Oregon. They've kept the kids for me so I could get down here."

"How'd you make it to Santa Barbara so quickly?" asked Tracy.

The attorney fielded this question. "Janet's family is very well off and they have their own jet. I work for the family and they called me immediately, not knowing any details. They didn't want her doing this alone and her father is too old to travel at this stage in his life. There's got to be more to this story than what you've told us so far. Please, tell us what is going on."

The detectives looked at each other as if to ask if the other wanted to tell them the rest of the story. Tracy, trying to be as sensitive as possible, started, "Mrs. Johnson, there is another element to this puzzle that we need to tell you about. There was another body found dead. A woman."

Janet looked up now with hurting eyes and a tear-soaked face. "What woman? Who is she? Was she found with my husband?" There were no more tears coming from her eyes. She anxiously waited for the detectives to fill her in.

"The woman was found dead in your bed at the house. We can only speculate at this point that it is related to your husband's death."

"In my bed?" Janet's hands came to her face as her head seem to collapse in them. "Who is she? How did she die? And what was she doing in my bed?"

"We really don't know much. There were no signs of what killed her," Detective Reynolds answered.

"Who is she?" Janet screamed.

"Her name is Jesse Anderson and she worked at the station." Detective Tracy passed a picture of Jesse across the table to Janet and her attorney as he spoke.

"Oh, god. God, god," Janet wept.

"Detectives, can we have a moment, please?" the attorney asked. The two detectives stood up and left the room.

Minutes later the door opened and Janet, held by the attorney, walked out. "I need to take Mrs. Johnson home to rest. Is there anything more you need from us right now?"

"No. We'll be in touch tomorrow. You will stay in town tonight, right?" asked detective Tracy.

"Yes, but probably not at the house. I don't think she wants to go there right now. Here's my card with my cell number on it. Please call me with any new details."

4

LISA HAD WATCHED the five and six o'clock newscasts on four monitors in her office. Every station, hers included, did live shots from the CBS 2 parking lot and from outside the Johnson house. There really wasn't anything new to report, but two dead bodies, one of whom was a TV news celebrity, was a big story in this coastal college town. All said the investigation into the causes of death was "ongoing." Reporters tried to get a comment from CBS 2, but Lisa declined, referring all questions to the police.

Lisa needed to head out to meet the owner of the station. She canceled her dinner plans with Tom, her husband. Nothing he wasn't use to. It was part of the business he married into. Tom was a successful radio manager for Clear Channel, but he knew in his heart that his wife's TV career was the predominant one in the family. He had done everything he could during their fourteen-year marriage to support her television career.

Station owner Stewart Simpson was seventy-two years old and a self-made multi-millionaire. He had once owned a chain of television and radio stations around the country. The CBS affiliate in Santa Barbara was his last one, having divested all the rest. He was known as a shrewd businessman who was a major player with the ladies. He was charming and kept himself in shape. Lisa had known Stewart twenty years, longer than anyone else at the station. She was twenty-five when she first met him.

She loved coming out to his Santa Barbara home located in the exclusive Home Ranch Estates. His home had five bedrooms, a guest house, and private access to the beach. It wasn't his main house, but he loved coming in from Dallas as much as possible.

Dugan met the car as Lisa pulled up the circular driveway. Dugan was Mr. Simpson's all around do-everything man—valet, superior executive chef, chauffer, personal confidant. Simpson trusted Dugan with everything inside and outside of his business—the women, the partying, the cheating on golf scores, everything. He was trusted as much as a man like Stewart Simpson could trust anyone.

"Good evening, Mrs. Campbell. It's good to see you again," Dugan greeted Lisa as he opened her car door.

"Dugan, you look good. Is he taking good care of you?" Dugan smiled at Lisa. They shared twenty years of secrets between them, and Lisa always felt only the two of them knew what the man was really about.

The door opened and Stewart was there with a glass of white wine for his general manager. They hugged and kissed, but it wasn't your typical peck on a cheek. This kiss was on the lips and there was more to it than a simple hello. "How are you?" she asked. "How was your trip?"

"No problems. Tell me what's going on. I couldn't figure out too much from the news tonight. What are we dealing with here?" Stewart Simpson got right to the point when it came to his business.

They walked into the living room. Lisa sat on the couch while Stewart sat on the foot stool in front of her. She quickly took off her heels and placed her legs under herself as she sat.

"We don't know what we have here. Steve, our anchor, was found dead sitting in his anchor chair on the news set. No obvious wounds and not even the rope around his neck proved to be anything. He was just dead. Then we found one of our newest employees, Jesse Anderson. She is actually an intern at the station. Jesse was found dead at Steve's house in his bed. Again, no obvious wounds to tell us what killed her. The coroner is doing autopsies tomorrow on both of them to determine the cause of death. What we can't figure out is the relationship between Steve and Jesse and why she was at his house when he was found at the station."

"How are your employees taking it? Anyone have anything? Someone has to know what is going on?" He reached out and began petting Lisa's foot that stuck out just enough for him to reach it.

"Our people seem to be okay. They're shocked, but doing okay. No one seems to know anything and everyone is speculating about this relationship between Steve and Jesse. Maybe there isn't a relationship. I don't know and at this point I'm exhausted trying to figure it out." Lisa took another drink of her wine.

"What about your news director? What's his name?" the owner asked.

"Barry Burke. He's been on top of this story all day and he seems as baffled as I am. He really doesn't seem to know anything and was as surprised as anyone about Jesse being in Steve's bed. In fact, he's the one that found her along with the police detective."

Lisa looks tired, Stewart thought.

Stewart reached his hand up from rubbing her foot, touching her arm. Then he gently touched her cheek, pulling her toward him. They kissed. She knew no one would understand their relationship and no one could ever find out. She was perfectly okay with what she was doing. Being held by Stewart and kissed by him right now was something she needed to make the events of the day disappear from her mind.

Tom never questioned his wife's time spent with the station owner. Stewart was very much part of her life when he met Lisa. Stewart had even paid for their very expensive wedding and gave them a luxurious honeymoon. Tom saw Lisa's relationship with Stewart as father-daughter. He chose not to ask beyond that, and the perks of her boss's relationship with his wife was worth not knowing, he thought.

***

The coroner was due to conduct his first autopsy at nine in the morning. No one from the outside was allowed to watch. Detectives Reynolds and Tracy were both there waiting in the office. The sooner they had a cause of death the sooner they could move this case along.

Barry was dealing with his newsroom. People were still positioning to take the number one male anchor chair. He'd even had a conversation last night with Angie, the co-anchor of the evening news. She wanted to suggest that she should solo anchor all the newscasts. Kind of like what CBS Network was doing with Katie Couric. The news director didn't say anything when this was suggested, but he thought, *Yeah, the Katie Couric move wouldn't be something I'd be bragging about at this point. So far it isn't a ringing success for the network.*

Dave Pedderman was holding court in the sales meeting down the hall from the general manager's office. Pedderman had been the general sales manager for four years, having been promoted to the position after Lisa advanced.

"What's the word on the street so far?" Pedderman asked his seven account executives gathered for a morning sales meeting.

"People seem to be in real shock. No one knows what to make of it. Is there anything we can tell them?" asked one of the staff.

"Not really. We don't know anything right now."

"The guys from ABC are already on the street talking trash about what happened," another staffer added. "They're asking their clients if they really want to be a part of such an operation associated with murder, sex, etcetera. Really low class."

"If we don't know anything, trust me when I tell you the other stations certainly don't know what is going on," Pedderman said. "Remind your clients of that. Let them know that we will share whatever we can when we have something. Take the high road on this. Don't get dragged into the gutter trying to defend ourselves. We truly don't know anything at this point."

"Hey, remind your clients now would be a great time to be advertising in our newscasts," another sales executive said. "Everyone in the market is going to be watching our stations because the story is about our people."

"That's a good point," Pedderman responded. "Make sure you get a premium on your local news rates."

The sales meeting broke up just in time for the department managers meeting, which Pedderman attended. Today's meeting would have a special guest—the owner. Stewart liked to pop into the station whenever he was in town so he could stay familiar with everyone. The managers never knew when he was going to show up, but they enjoyed him whenever he did. He was stopping by today to try to calm everyone's nerves.

Stewart Simpson arrived looking tanned, fit, and impeccably dressed. He was once married, but when that ended in an expensive divorce he swore off the institution. It was probably a good thing considering his active sex life that never showed signs of slowing. Maybe he used Viagra. Maybe it was something that money and power gave a person like him. Whatever the reason for his youthfulness, he went through life at his own pace and at his own pleasure.

The downside to these pop-in visits was that he never seemed satisfied with the station's financial performance. He wasn't shy about speaking up and letting people who worked for him know it, either.

"Good morning, everyone." Lisa hadn't even introduced him yet. He just walked in the room and took charge. "Dave, where's my money?" he asked General Sales Manager David Pedderman. Then turning to the news director, "Barry, you really screwed us on that live shot yesterday morning."

Barry was caught off guard, as was Lisa. One by one, Stewart went department by department to take his piece of hide. The whole cycle took about forty-five minutes.

"Look, what happened yesterday was a tragedy on so many levels. Some of you were very close with Steve. Did anyone know this new girl?" The room was silent, filled with looks going from one person to another to see if anyone would answer the question. No one did.

"We have to remain true to ourselves. You have to be supportive to this station, where you work, and to those that you work with. Do not get caught up in all the gossip and bullshit. We are in this together and we will survive together. I appreciate your continued hard work." And with that he exited the room like he came in. Lisa wrapped the meeting up and quickly stepped into the hall to find the owner.

She didn't like Stewart walking the halls by himself. You never knew who would confront him and start talking about who knew what. Why put him in that situation? Hell, why create that situation for yourself? Her job, as long as he was going to be in the station, would be to ride shotgun wherever he went so she could protect him, herself, and the employees.

Barry left the meeting, and as soon as he got in the hallway, he tried reaching his friend. "You know anything yet?"

"Coroner is still working on Steve. I'll call you as soon as I have something for you. I promise," the detective replied.

"You have to have something. Can you at least tell me how he died?"

"Barry, we haven't found anything yet, as far as I know. It looks like natural causes. The rope doesn't appear to have anything to do with his death. Hell, there wasn't even any bruising on his neck. I'll get back to you."

John Rankin, the young assignment editor who found Steve dead in the studio, was knocking on the news director's door just as Barry ended his call with the detective. "What do you need, John?" Barry stood behind his desk looking over some papers.

"Mr. Burke, can I talk to you a minute?"

"Yeah, grab a chair." Barry took a seat as well. "What's on your mind?"

"I know you have a lot on your plate and I'm not sure the best time to bring this up."

Barry cut him off quickly. "John, get to the point. What do you want?"

"I want to report. I want to get on the street and do some reporting. That's what I've always wanted."

"What?" The news director liked the balls on this kid. "John, why today? Why is this important right now?"

"I don't want to seem insensitive, but I'm afraid if I sit on the sidelines and don't say anything then I might miss an opportunity." John's confidence was building.

"What chance? Am I looking for a new reporter right now?"

"I thought with the loss of Jesse, and her being new and a reporter-in-training, her spot might need to be filled. I want to have that spot."

Barry rubbed his head; he liked the way this kid was

thinking. A brazen go-getter. He's perfect for the news game, Barry thought.

"John, interesting idea. If we decide to fill the slot I will give you some consideration. Right now I need you to jump on that desk and hold it down for us. Okay?" Barry stood as a sign the meeting was over. John stood up and Barry shook John's hand and basically did everything but lead him out the door.

"Thanks, Mr. Burke. I appreciate your consideration. Thank you." And with that John went back to his assignment desk.

Dave Pedderman and Rick Hansen passed John leaving Barry's office and proceeded to step in and sit down before Barry could get behind his desk. "Any time the two of you show up together usually means trouble. What do I owe this visit to?" Barry asked.

"We're thinking we should make Steve Johnson's funeral a huge deal. He's been the top anchor in this area longer than anyone else. He is respected by everyone in the community, and this would be a great way for us to milk this for a while." The sales manager was about as insensitive as anyone in the building. It was always about revenue.

Barry jumped out of his seat and got to his door as quickly as possible to shut it. He didn't want any employees hearing this morbid conversation about how the station could generate positive ratings from a tragic event.

"Milk this for a while?" Barry repeated back to the two sitting across from him.

Pedderman continued. "We think we could get a couple of hours of programming out of this. I'm sure I could get the business community to pay a hefty premium to sponsor coverage of his funeral. We might even consider coming up with a one-hour special on the life of Steve Johnson."

"Wow! Really? Are you two fucking serious? I'm not even sure what I'm to make of this." Looking into their eyes, Barry could tell, so he said it. "You two are fucking serious, aren't you?"

"We are. We are serious about this. Think about it. This is a well-respected man in the community who has been the number one news anchor for more than ten years. He has incredible ratings and has always had incredible ratings. Let's recognize the opportunity for what it is," Pedderman insisted.

"He has done so much in this community that the community will want to say goodbye," the promotion manager added.

"You want to capitalize on his death and do what? Maybe have his replacement do the eulogy as a way to introduce him or her to our audience?" Barry wasn't sure what to think.

"We hadn't thought about that angle, but that is good. If we know his replacement, that would be a nice touch that probably no one would really pick up on." Pedderman's sense of humor was something Barry hadn't gotten used to, but even this was going beyond his own sense of poor taste.

"If you guys are really serious and you think we should do something as a station, then we need to get Lisa involved." Barry reached over to his phone and hit Lisa's intercom button.

"This is Lisa."

"Lisa, Barry. I've got Dave and Rick in here. Do you have a minute to meet with us?"

"I'll be right down."

"Hi, guys. What's up?" she asked as she entered the room.

Pedderman began. "We thought it would be a good idea if the station did something special on the funeral for Steve Johnson. And maybe even create a half-hour retrospective look at Steve's life and his contribution to Santa Barbara."

Lisa listened and then thought about it for a few minutes. "I like the idea about the half-hour special. That would be a nice touch. We could do it as told through the people in the newsroom who worked with Steve." She looked at Barry, trying to gauge his receptiveness to the idea.

Lisa continued. "I'd be worried about doing anything at the funeral. We don't want to take anything away from the family and we don't know what their plans are yet. It's still too new. And before we do anything with a special, we need to make sure we don't have something here that is going to blow up into some huge scandal."

Barry interjected. "Let's start working on the special and putting the pieces together. The news department can start doing the work and that way we're ahead of the game if we decide to move forward. I agree with Lisa that we need to make sure we don't have some kind of freakish thing going on before we do too much celebrating of his life."

The phone rang in Barry's office. Recognizing the number that popped up, he asked everyone if they could step out of the room.

"Richard, what do you have? Is the autopsy done?"

"The coroner is done with Steve. He'll start on Jesse after lunch. We don't really have anything that helps us right now. It looks as though he died of natural causes. No damage to his organs out of the ordinary. No puncture wounds. No bullet holes. No sign of a drug overdose or poisoning. This one is very puzzling to everyone working it. We don't have a real cause of death. Yet he was sitting in a chair with a rope around his neck as if he'd been hanged."

"How can that be, Richard? What about the contents of his stomach? Any traces of anything out of the ordinary?" Barry asked his detective friend.

"That's what I'm telling you. The coroner hasn't discovered anything to this point. I'll call you again once he's opened up Jesse."

Barry went down the hall and filled Lisa in, who in turn went to tell Stewart. She drove out to his place at Home Ranch Estates for a planned pleasure lunch meeting.

* * *

Stewart was in the Jacuzzi overlooking the Pacific Ocean. Lisa walked through the house, out the back door, and dropped a piece of clothing with every step. At forty-five, Lisa was a beautiful, well-preserved brunette with very toned legs and arms. She wasn't shy about her body as she confidently stepped into the hot water, taking Stewart's hand. The two embraced and kissed before sitting down.

"No one can figure this one out. No signs of any foul play, and yet Steve died in a very weird way. I also haven't found out anything that would lead me to believe Steve was cheating on his wife with this girl Jesse."

"What about the girl Jesse?" Stewart asked. "What's her story?"

"We really don't know anything. She's only been at the station three weeks. She moved here from somewhere in Texas. I talked to her dad but he didn't indicate anything in our conversation. It's hard to know how to feel because we don't know anything."

Stewart handed Lisa a glass of wine. Normally she wouldn't drink during the day, but when she was with Stewart she had no rules. "Have the families made any funeral arrangements?" He seemed legitimately concerned for his two dead employees.

"I don't think anyone has made any arrangements as yet. I would imagine that Jesse's body will be sent back to Texas where her family is. I haven't talked to Steve's wife since we met her at the police station. I don't know where her head is at."

Lisa was relaxing for the first time in several days. It would be hard not to relax sitting in the hot, bubbly water overlooking the Pacific Ocean while drinking a glass of wine. This was exactly what she needed, and Stewart knew that. He also knew she needed one more thing, and he slowly held her and pulled her on top of him. She lost herself in the passion of the moment, and she felt safe in Stewart's grasp. Lunch was over and Lisa grabbed the robe towel that Dugan had left for her on the lounge chair as she got out of the Jacuzzi. Stewart followed, putting on his own robe.

"Some of the department heads think we should do a half-hour special celebrating Steve's contributions to Santa Barbara and the area," Lisa said.

"Is that what you want to do?"

"I'm not sure, Stewart. I think it's too premature to do anything until we know what we're dealing with. The last thing we want to do is celebrate his life and then find out he was killed because he was having an affair or maybe something worse."

"Good girl. I've taught you well. No need to rush into anything right now. Make sure we find out all the facts before we start down a road we may not want to go down. Also, I want to cover all the costs of the funerals. I don't want anyone to know, but I don't want the families to be out of pocket on something like this."

Janet took a step over and kissed her boss's cheek. She was touched by his generosity but never surprised by it. This was something she had seen time and time again.

***

The widow Janet Johnson hung up the phone after speaking to Detective Reynolds. She walked into the small living room that was part of her suite at the hotel and sat down. Her attorney, Byron Culpepper, had decided to stay at the hotel the previous night to keep an eye on Janet. She didn't want to go to the house partly because she was scared, partly because of the dead body, and partly because she was pissed at the thought her husband had cheated on her. And there was the press, everywhere. Not to mention it was an active crime scene. Janet couldn't understand what was going on around her. She was lost and confused and worried about her three daughters. Yes, her family was wealthy, so she didn't have to worry about money. But that was little comfort when her loving family life was disappearing all around her.

"What did the police say?" her attorney asked.

"Not really anything. He told me that the coroner worked on Steve this morning and the findings were inconclusive. In other words, they didn't find anything."

"Okay. What about the autopsy on the girl? Have they learned anything there?" The attorney was trying to get as much information as possible so he could help his client and family friend.

"After lunch. After lunch the coroner will begin that autopsy. Maybe that will tell them something." Janet started sobbing.

The attorney walked over and led her over to the couch, placing a blanket over her body. "Rest." Byron Culpepper was a well-known private practice attorney with a handful of clients. Janet's family was one of them. He knew what he had to do and began the ball rolling by placing a cell phone call to the firm's in-house investigator.

"Johnny, I need a complete background check into Steve Johnson. Yes, he's Janet's husband. I need to know everything this guy was up to for the past two years. Find out everything you can and let's update his file. Then check on a girl by the name of Jesse Anderson. I want to know if Steve was banging this girl. Get on it right away and let me know what you come up with." Culpepper wanted to get out in front of whatever he might be dealing with.

One of the jobs Culpepper did for wealthy clients was to thoroughly check out anyone who came into their families. His firm had done a complete background check on Steve Johnson before Janet married him. Culpepper was being extra cautious and wanted to go over his complete background again. It's not normal for people to just turn up dead. If something was going to come out, he wanted to know it first.

* * *

The newsroom was busy getting ready for the five o'clock newscast. Billie Latzke would anchor the news by herself as she did the night before. Billie was a strikingly beautiful blonde who dressed to the nines and had been co-anchoring the evening news with Steve Johnson for the past six years. She wasn't the best reader of news but her looks brought in viewers of all types. Even the women of Santa Barbara and surrounding areas liked to look at her.

The death of her co-anchor affected her differently than most might expect. The two anchors had sat next to each other for three newscasts a night for six years. They were more professional acquaintances than friends. It was rough in the beginning and there was occasional flirting between the two that never developed into anything. The flirting from Billie's side came out of nervousness for wanting to please the number one male anchor, who she believed could take her job if he didn't like her. His flirting was more of a defensive move because of her beauty. He was like the little boy who didn't know how to let the little girl know he liked her. Their purely professional relationship made them a stronger team on air.

Billie always came in and did her job. She didn't try to mix it up with the others in the newsroom. She wanted to do her job well every single night. No one really socialized with her outside the station, so her private life remained very private. That suited Billie just fine.

"Barry, you got a minute?" Billie asked, standing at his door.

"Come in, Billie. Everything okay?" Barry felt very close to all his anchors, especially his core team. He brought Billie on six years ago when the main female anchor spot opened up. She was brought in from the San Francisco market where she was trying to break in as a reporter. It was hard for a new reporter to get face time in a top-five market without on-air experience. Billie came out of USC's Annenberg School of Journalism and was lucky enough to land a paid internship in the Bay area, but that was because of her looks. The bottom line was that she wasn't going to get any real face time until she honed her skills in a smaller market.

One of the news producers Barry knew at the station in San Francisco tipped him off about the new, gorgeous news girl. Barry called her and asked her to come to Santa Barbara and audition. She got the gig.

"I just wanted to check to see how you are doing. You've had some pretty tough days. You okay?" Billie always took the time to get a read on Barry's pulse. He appreciated it when one of his troops asked how he was doing. He thought it meant they cared, at least a little.

"I'm good. Say, do you know anything about Steve or this new girl Jesse that could help us figure out what was going on?"

"No. I know Steve was spending some time with her working on her reading and how to punch up a story. He was working with her on that kind of stuff, but I don't think he really had much to do with her outside the station."

"So why do you think she was found dead in his bed, at his house, when his wife was away?"

"I guess if you figure that one out you will answer the mystery."

"What mystery is that, Billie? You said it would answer the mystery. What mystery?"

"Why, who killed them," she responded.

"You're probably right. That's why we have detectives, though. Hey, I'm thinking about giving the kid on the assignment desk, John, a shot at reporting. We're down one reporter with Jesse being . . ." he hesitated saying the word. "Any thoughts about that idea?"

"I don't really know him. He seems like a good kid. He's usually out of the office by the time I come in at two," Billie said.

"Well, don't say anything. I might give him a try. On another subject, I'm not sure how we're going to fill Steve's position right now. As you can imagine, everyone has come in here to pitch the position. It hasn't even been two days yet," Barry said in a somewhat disappointed voice.

"I know, but you know how news people are. They feel if they don't speak up as soon as a spot opens up it might disappear under their nose. Are you thinking about someone on staff?" she asked.

"Don't know, to be honest. I'm not sure we have anyone who is strong enough. Jake wants the opportunity, but he's good in the morning and that would just open up another area that I'd have to fill. Carlos put in his two cents, but he's not ready. It might serve us well to go outside the market and bring in a new look."

"What about Phil Roberts over on ABC?" Billie asked.

"I hadn't thought about him. He's probably under contract, I would think."

"He might be, but maybe they don't use contracts. I know him if you want me to give him a call to feel him out," Billie offered.

"It wouldn't hurt to find out if he has any interest. Don't go out of your way, but if you talk to him, run it by him to see if he's interested, Barry suggested.

Billie left and Barry was pleased because he got out of that conversation exactly what he'd intended. He knew about the relationship with her competitor, Phil Roberts. More to the point, he was aware of her relationship with Stephanie Roberts, Phil's sister. It was never talked about or discussed, and Barry was sure no one in his newsroom was aware of Billie's relationship.

Barry's cell buzzed.

"Barry, it's Richard. I'm at the autopsy for Jesse Anderson. You're not going to believe this. The coroner can't find any reason for death. No presence of drugs. No gunshot wounds or stab wounds. No signs of a struggle of any kind. The lab has sent the blood work up so we'll see what that comes back. And get this. There are no signs of any sexual activity before she died. None! What do you make of this? I thought at the very least we'd find the two had sex that night. We're not even sure if they saw each other that evening."

"Richard, what are you saying? You think it's possible this girl ended up in Steve's bed, at his house, dead, and they might not have even seen each other that night? How is that possible?"

"Believe me, we are all baffled by this. The department hasn't been able to turn up one link to these two victims other than the girl ended up dead in his bed. There doesn't seem to be anything tying these two together the night they died. And the coroner can't tell us yet how they died or what they died from."

"Is he thinking possibly a double suicide?" Barry asked.

"No. He doesn't believe it was suicide, either. Barry, he doesn't know and we don't even have a theory at this point. I just wanted to give you the information as I got it. I need to call the girl's family. Remember, this is an on-going investigation so this information is not being released to the public. You certainly can't put it in your newscast. Don't screw me on this."

"Okay, Richard. But I've got to do reporting on this story. It's huge, and I know my competitors are all over it. We're going to keep on it. My people will file a request for the coroner's findings through proper police channels. We've got to do our jobs here."

"I understand, Barry. But you can't use the information I gave you and you can't use me as a source. Got it?"

Barry wanted to talk to Lisa to discuss putting their own investigative reporters on the story, someone to independently ferret out information on the case. The station had resources that could possibly help the police.

"Lisa, it's Barry. My hands are tied regarding autopsy information. The coroner found nothing on either body, but I can't disclose the results. I think we need to do our own investigation and put someone on this story full time."

"Have you discussed this with Richard or Skip at the police department yet?" Lisa asked.

"Yes, I told Richard we needed to keep reporting on this story, that it's big news, and I promised not to reveal any information he provided me."

"What do you think you're going to find that the police won't? Or maybe the better question is, what do you hope to find?"

"I don't know what we'll find. Something isn't right. There are no obvious motives or even crimes that anyone can tell right now. No weapons. We really just have two dead bodies and they both work for us."

"We have a new employee found dead in the bed of our main anchor is what we have."

"Yes, Lisa, but no one can tell us why. No one can tell us even if they were fucking each other." Barry looked quickly to the door to make sure it was closed. "I don't know what we're going to find, but let's find out. What can it hurt? We won't get in the way of the police work. I'll share everything we get with the investigating detectives. Let me put a couple of people on this to see what we come up with. I won't even tell our own people that we are doing an investigation. I'll assign stories to different reporters as if they are side bars to the police investigation."

"That will work for me. If you promise to handle it like that, I can be okay with it. I don't want you coming out at the end of all this with a three-piece murder special report. I won't be happy if that is your goal."

***

Barry began formulating a plan as soon as he ended his call with Lisa. He thought that maybe he might take the lead on this one himself. He missed working a beat and turning great stories. This might be a perfect one to rekindle his fire. The news department was young and inexperienced at investigative reporting. Some of the people could take parts of this and that way it wouldn't look like a major investigative piece. Carlos Hernandez could take one part. Carlos was the most seasoned reporter on the staff.

Barry immediately started planning his strategy and the main questions that needed to be answered. Perhaps the most intriguing: Why was Jesse Anderson in Steve Johnson's bed?

5

JANET JOHNSON WANTED her husband's body released for burial. The police investigation wouldn't allow that to happen until after they were sure they had everything they needed. They decided they wanted to hold the body until the lab work came back. It would only be another day or two. Meanwhile, the investigation had turned to background checks into Steve Johnson's family. The police wanted to know what kind of marriage Steve and Janet had. Were there problems in the marriage? What they really wanted to find out was if Janet had any motive to kill her husband.

The obvious motive was this relationship with Jesse Anderson, the dead girl found in the wife's bed. What was her relationship to Steve? Until that question was answered there wasn't anything to point to Janet, at least for now. Money was not the issue, according to bank records. Janet had a family trust that pretty much set her up for life. There was a standard life insurance policy from the station that provided the beneficiary one and half times the employee's salary. In the scheme of things for Janet, that really didn't amount to very much.

Janet received visits from friends and station people most of day two. Her family flew down and brought a nanny with them to watch the three girls. Janet still had not gone back to the house. The family had gotten a couple of suites at the Marriott to stay secluded from news reporters.

Billie Latzke, Steve's co-anchor, showed up at the hotel around eleven to pay her respects to Janet. They had known each other ever since Billie became the co-anchor six years ago. Janet was surprised to see Billie but accepted her guest with a hug.

"Janet, I don't even know what to say. It's such a loss for all of us," Billie said to the new widow.

Janet realized that Billie's pain was real. She knew there was never anything between her husband and the pretty anchor woman. It was nice to have this intimate moment with her. The two stood there for a few minutes just holding each other's arms. There were tears but no real crying.

"Is there anything I can do for you, Janet?" Billie asked.

"Go for a ride with me. I need to get out of here for a few minutes," Janet said in an almost desperate tone. Billie was surprised but felt she had no choice.

"Let's go," she said.

"I need to go by the house and pick up a few things," Janet told Billie.

"Not a problem. Just tell me how to get there." It had dawned on both women that in the past six years Billie had never been invited to their house.

The ride over was quiet. Janet just wanted some company. It didn't matter that she didn't really have a relationship with Billie. It was probably easier that they weren't best friends. Janet stared out the window and then asked the question Billie didn't want to hear.

"Was Steve fucking that girl?"

"Janet, I honestly don't believe Steve ever slept around on you—with anyone—at least not to my knowledge. Steve and I worked well together, but we were not really close, at least personally. We talked about work, but not much more."

Billie didn't know for sure, but that is how she felt after six years sitting next to this man. He never showed any signs of screwing around on his wife.

"I was baffled when I heard about the girl being found in your bed. It certainly raises questions, but I honestly don't believe that Steve did anything with that girl."

The new widow started sobbing. The cries were slow and heartbreaking. Nothing else was said the rest of the drive to the house.

***

Yellow crime scene tape blocked off the front door and was also visible on the gate to the backyard. The police had locked up the house but Janet had her key. The two women didn't worry about breaking the tape on the porch. Janet wasn't too concerned about anything at this point and just crossed through the barrier and unlocked the door. The house was as she had left it. Nothing was disturbed or out of place except for the noticeable mess in the master bedroom where the girl was found. Janet seemed to stand at the foot of the bed for the longest time. Billie stood behind her and patted her shoulder for support.

Janet asked for Billie's help as she walked over to the bed and began to lift the mattress off the box spring.

"Janet, what are you doing? I'm not sure the police want us to touch anything," Billie said in a shocked kind of tone.

"Help me, Billie." The two carried the mattress out the back door, sheets and all, and placed it in the backyard. They then walked back into the house and did the same thing with the box spring. Billie could only imagine what Janet was feeling. Once they placed the box spring somewhat on top of the mattress, Billie turned to go back into the house. Janet didn't follow. Instead, Janet went to the door leading to the garage and disappeared for a brief minute. She came out carrying a can of lighter fluid, which she opened and emptied onto the mattress and box spring set. Billie watched as Janet then walked in the back door and over to the stove. She took the newspaper that was on the kitchen counter, rolled it up, lit it, and walked her torch out to the backyard and dropped it on the pile. The bed went up in flames.

6

BARRY CALLED HIS young assignment editor John into his office. He wanted to take his pulse before offering him a chance to begin his news reporting career. The news director wanted to be sure he was up to the task.

"Sit down, John. How are you?"

"I'm good. Why?" he questioned out loud.

"You've been through quite a bit the last couple of days and I wanted to make sure you were okay. I want to give you an opportunity to do some reporting. Be careful what you ask for. Are you up for this?" Barry asked John.

John's eyes widened. "Yes, sir. I'm up for it."

"Let's see what you got. I want you to work some background on this Steve and Jesse story. We need to know if there was anything romantic or otherwise between the two of them. We need to piece together the timeline between when Steve got off the eleven o'clock news until you found him in the studio just before three. Basically, we need to find out everything you can that might help us know what happened so we can report it."

John thought this was an awful lot to give such a cub reporter. Then again, he was sure others in the newsroom were working on other parts of this story.

"Mr. Burke, what about the assignment desk? Do you still want me to work that as well?" John asked his boss.

"No, John. I'm going to ask Tami, the intern, to take that job for now. Starting tomorrow, I want you as one of my reporters. That means I need at least one story out of you every day for the newscasts. Your work on this investigation piece will have to be separate. You have to show me everything that you come up with every day so we can compare notes with what everyone else has."

"Not a problem, boss." John left the office without touching the floor.

Barry knew he had lots to uncover. How did she get to Steve's bed? Had they met after the eleven o'clock news was over? Why was she in his bed if they didn't have sex? There were so many questions that didn't make sense. He pushed the intercom button to buzz the station's IT guy.

"Rex, I need you to direct all of Steve Johnson's emails for the past thirty days over to me. I also want to see anything Jesse Anderson was doing as well. Thanks."

Barry thought maybe he'd get lucky and find something in an email that might explain their relationship. Right now, he had nothing. Next up was a trip to the business office located on the other side of the building. The news department had its own little wing of the building. That separated news from the sales guys. It was an unwritten rule that news and sales should not mingle. The news guys worried about "news integrity." Sales people never thought about that side of things. What was the problem if McDonald's wanted to show their new morning coffee off by having their McDonald's coffee cups on the morning show anchor desk? Revenue seemed to always trump "news integrity."

Barry next called a business manager to get the phone records for the past sixty days on Steven Johnson's phone. "Did we pay for his cell phone? If so, I'll need his cell phone records as well."

"I should have these things by this afternoon," the business manager said. The entire conversation took less than a minute and Barry was headed back to his office.

Billie was waiting for Barry. She wanted to tell her boss about her outing with Janet Johnson and the burning of the bed. As he listened to her describe the incident, he quietly wondered if the police were done with the bed. If not, Steve's wife might have ruined some evidence.

"Billie, it sounds like you had a fun time. Have you talked to the police yet?"

"I talked to them only briefly, but they're supposed to contact me again to follow up," Billie answered.

"What happened that last night Steve was on the air with you? Was Steve acting funny about anything? We're trying to figure out what he did from the time the eleven o'clock news was over until John found him in the studio."

"Barry, it was a typical night in the newsroom. There wasn't anything going on. We even joked about it being a real slow news day. I do remember he took two or three calls between ten and the start of the newscast. That was a little out of the norm. Steve never got a lot of phone calls that late in the night. I figured at least one of the calls was Janet checking in. Then it didn't seem like he was talking to Janet after that."

"Why do say that?" Barry asked.

"It was the way he was talking on the phone."

"You think it might have been Jesse calling?" Barry wondered.

"No, I don't think so. And Barry, I really don't think Steve was doing anything with Jesse outside of the station."

"Then why was she found dead in his bed? Do you know where Steve went after the newscast was over?"

"I assumed he just went home. In hindsight I haven't any idea," Billie said.

"Okay, you need to start working on tonight's newscast. I've got to make a few phone calls. Shut my door, please." Billie went to her desk area and Barry got on the phone and called Tracy.

"Yeah, Barry, I was just going to call you. We got the coroner reports back. You want to see them?"

"Anything new turn up?"

"No, it's like I told you earlier. No cause of death has been determined. Come down and take a look for yourself."

"I'm on my way." Barry grabbed his cigarettes off his desk and out the door he went.

The drive from the station to the police department was twenty minutes. The ride seemed like only minutes because his thoughts were occupied by every possible twist he could imagine. Who else was involved? If it was somebody at the station, he wondered if anyone else was in danger. He thought the station should hire a security guard to be on the premises in the evening. Barry would bring that up to Lisa later that day.

Barry pulled into the Santa Barbara police station. He had to sign in at the front desk while waiting for detectives Tracy and Reynolds to come get him.

"You want coffee or anything before we sit down?" Tracy asked.

"No, I'm good. So, the autopsy turned up nothing?"

"Honestly, Barry, it's like nothing I've ever seen before. The coroner didn't find anything. The blood work came back and there was nothing." Reynolds and Tracy were shaking their heads.

"That's bizarre," Barry said. "Something killed them."

"That's just it. We have nothing. Don't you think that is extremely odd? The coroner has come up empty," Detective Reynolds said.

"So, what's next, then? Where do you go from here? Did he test for poison?" Barry asked.

"I would assume so, but let's call him and see." Tracy picked up the phone and dialed the coroner's direct line.

"Samuels," the coroner answered.

"Yeah, this is Richard Tracy. Did you run tests for poisons and all that good stuff on the Johnson and Anderson bodies?"

"That's what we're going to do now," he replied.

"Why wasn't that part of the original autopsy? I thought you told me you ruled out poisoning," Reynolds said.

"The original autopsy is performed looking for normal causes of death. We didn't have any reason to test for poisons or anything like that when we started."

"What did you find that leads you to believe you should test for poisons now?" Barry asked.

"The fact that we didn't find anything else to point to cause of death is the reason we need to go back in and check for other signs now," the coroner explained.

"What about their internal organs?" Barry asked. "Any signs there that would indicate any foul play?"

"No. Guys, I wish I had something for you, but I don't. You have my report. We didn't find anything that would tell us why these two people died two days ago. When I run these new tests, I will let you know what we find."

"Barry, has your team turned up anything?" Tracy asked.

"Not a thing right yet. We're just getting started. What are we missing here?" Barry asked the detectives.

"Let's talk about what we know. So far we've been talking about what we don't know. Let's talk about what we know." Richard Tracy got some chalk from his desk drawer and walked over to the blackboard.

Reynolds started. "We know that the two people who died worked together."

"We know Steve got off work between eleven thirty-five when the newscast ended and eleven forty-five," Barry added.

"The coroner did determine the time of death was between one and two in the morning," Tracy said.

"Wait a minute," Reynold said as if he had finally found something. "What was the time of death for Jesse? What did the coroner say about the girl's death?

Tracy flipped the pages from his clipboard. "Here it is. Her time of death was also between one and two."

"That means they could have been together then," Barry said confidently.

"Why? Why does that tell us they were together?" Tracy questioned. "This only gives us their approximate time of death. It doesn't tell us anything else right now. It does appear that they both died apparently about the same time."

"You're right. I just assumed that if they both died at the same time they had to be together."

"Barry, has anyone at the station mentioned anything about Steve and Jesse seeing each other?" Reynolds asked.

"I've talked to most of the people in the station that have anything to do with this investigation and no one even believes Steve ever had a relationship with Jesse. Nothing points us there. She's only been at our station for three weeks or so."

"This only makes sense if the two were seeing each other. Then we have motive from several different places. Steve might have killed Jesse because she threatened to go to his wife about them. Maybe Jesse killed Steve because he wouldn't leave his wife. Then to make a statement she killed herself in Steve and Janet's bed." Reynolds was on a roll and neither Barry nor Tracy wanted to slow him down. "She wasn't pregnant or that would have shown up in the autopsy."

"What if Steve's wife found out and killed both of them?" Tracy had thought this before but had never said it out loud. "Or maybe her family had them killed. They have enough money they could pay someone to have done this." Tracy really didn't believe that, but it was another option. "You know Janet did show up with an attorney the first time we met here."

There was a slight silence as everyone in the room contemplated the different scenarios that were just laid out. Barry was first to speak. "I don't think Janet knew anything about Jesse."

"What do you base that on?" asked Reynolds.

"Her reaction when she was told what happened. Maybe it's a gut feeling. I'm not sure, but she seemed to be hearing these things about Jesse for the first time." Barry wished he had more, but that was all he had to go on. "Have the two of you interviewed her yet?"

"No, and we need to do that right away. We were waiting for the coroner's report because we wanted to be able to tell her how Steve died."

"Maybe she already knows," Reynolds quipped.

***

Forty-five minutes later, the attorney and Janet Johnson came into the police station. This time they were taken to an interview room and not the conference room. The detectives wanted to make it a little more intimidating. The interview room had a recorder set up on the table with a table microphone. This would be an official interview.

Byron had informed Janet that things might be different this time around when they met with the detectives. Janet was beginning to feel more like a client than friend to Byron. The first thing the police always do in a suspicious death of a spouse is try to rule out the other spouse as quickly as possible. More times than not the spouse did it. The detectives were thinking it was time to try and rule Janet out as a suspect. It didn't matter that Janet was in Bend, Oregon, at the time, or appeared to be. They'd have to confirm her alibi. They already saw how fast travel can be when you have daddy's jet. These were some of the issues that needed to be cleared up.

The four sat down at the table. The two detectives sat on one side of the table and the attorney and his client on the other side. They exchanged pleasantries and then Reynolds politely asked, "Are you alright if we record this conversation? It makes it easier for our record keeping."

The attorney had been through these types of questioning a hundred times in his career. His client list, although small, always seemed to be in one type of litigation or another.

"We're okay with the recording, but this is beginning to feel more like an interrogation than interview. Now you know why the family wanted me to be here with Janet."

The detectives looked at each other. They understood what the attorney was saying. "Let's begin," and with that Tracy reached over and turned on the recorder. "This is an interview with Janet Johnson. Present in the room are her attorney Byron Culpepper, police Detective Skip Reynolds and I am Detective Richard Tracy. It is three fifteen on October 12. Mrs. Johnson, where were you on the night your husband was found dead?"

That didn't take long. They just get right to the point, Janet thought. She looked at her attorney, who gave her a nod as if it was okay to answer. It was obvious that she had been coached. "I was visiting my parent's home in Bend, Oregon."

"How did you find out about Steve's death?" Detective Tracy asked.

"I was told by Lisa Campbell, the station general manager."

"Did she call you or did you call her?" Tracy followed up.

"She first called and left me a message. When I returned her call, she told me about Steve."

"Did she tell you about Jesse Anderson, too?" asked Reynolds.

"No, I don't believe so." Janet then remembered the initial meeting with the two detectives and added, "No. She didn't tell me about Jesse Anderson. You told me about Jesse the day I first met with you."

"Do you know who Jesse Anderson is?" Reynolds asked.

"I know now. At the time I didn't know who she was."

"Gentlemen," the attorney broke in, "are you thinking my client had something to do with her spouse's death? Are you treating her as a suspect?"

Tracy answered. "We don't know. Our goal is to eliminate her as a suspect. Right now we don't have anything to work with except a husband and his co-worker who are dead. The co-worker was found in his bed—their bed. If his wife knew or thought something was going on between them, then maybe she took matters into her own hands."

"We want to cooperate, but Janet Johnson is not a hostile witness. She wants to find the answers as well. Let's keep this as polite as possible and be sensitive that she just lost her husband and is still in shock."

Reynolds picked up the questioning. "Janet, have you been back to the house in the last twenty-four hours or so?"

The attorney didn't understand the question because he thought he had been with Janet the whole time she'd been in Santa Barbara. His client's answer caught him off guard.

"Yes. I have been to the house, once. I needed to pick some things up."

"And while you were there, did you do anything else besides pick some things up?" Reynolds knew the answer before she replied.

"I set my bed on fire." Janet wasn't showing any emotion when answering the detective.

"Didn't you see the crime tape around the door saying, 'Do not enter?' Didn't you think under the circumstances that the bed might be needed as evidence?" Reynolds asked.

Quietly, with her head down, Janet mustered an answer. "I didn't care. I just wanted to burn the bed. I couldn't stand the idea that my husband and this whore might have had sex in my bed. I just wanted to burn the bed." Janet was becoming upset.

"Look, can we take a break or come back tomorrow? Janet is overwhelmed with all of this." The attorney knew it was a long shot. Why would the detectives want to let her off the hook at this point when they'd gotten her so emotional?

"Just a few more questions before we let you go. Did you kill your husband or Jesse Anderson?' Tracy asked.

She didn't answer. All she could do was look up, and she started sobbing. The detectives thought she might be trying to buy some time, but they were wrong. Maybe she was overcome by guilt, they thought. They were wrong again.

"We're done here," said Byron Culpepper. "We'll be glad to come back at another time to answer any more questions, but we're done right now. My client is too distraught to continue." The attorney stood and led his client by her arm, and out the door they went.

The detectives stayed back in the room for a few moments. "What do you think?" asked Reynolds.

"I think she didn't know anything about the other woman. I don't think she did it, and we still don't have anything tying the two dead people together."

"Yes, we do," Tracy said. "We have a dead girl found in Janet and Steve Johnson's bed. There is a connection. We just haven't figured out what it is."

7

BARRY GOT BACK to his place to find the lights on and a wonderful meal waiting for him. Tami, the intern, was showing her culinary skills, something he hadn't seen before. He was wondering if she was getting too comfortable with their secret relationship. It was inappropriate on so many levels, but specifically from a human resources standpoint at the station. Barry knew he could lose his job if his boss, Lisa, ever got wind of it.

Tami was in her senior year at USC. This was her third year interning at the Santa Barbara affiliate. Nothing romantic occurred between her and Barry those first two summers at the station, but this summer she pursued him and Barry took the bait. He still couldn't understand what she saw in him, but he was tired of being alone, and it didn't matter to him anymore what her reason was. He liked it and the relationship had been easy so far. He wondered if things were changing because she was making him dinner.

"What's the occasion?" Barry asked as he came through the door.

"I just thought with everything going on you needed a good, home-cooked meal," Tami said as she greeted Barry with a kiss.

She wasn't wrong. The past couple of days had been nonstop

and Barry wasn't sure when it would end. He loved it when work was like this, but he was no longer in his thirties. He wasn't in his forties. Time had a way of catching up with news directors and Barry was starting to feel it. Tami made him feel young. She was five feet six inches tall with long legs—a looker, which would serve her well in the news business.

Their relationship started out innocently enough. Then one day she boldly told Barry she was interested in him. During her first two years interning with Barry she learned a lot, but she was feeling an attraction for her boss that went beyond a mentor-student relationship. When summer ended, she sat her boss down and told him how she felt. Barry didn't accept it right away, although he wanted to. He knew it could be hazardous to his employment. He'd been down that road before. Tami persisted and even presented a plan. She would take the first semester of the new school year off and stay in Santa Barbara to be with Barry. She would continue earning some college credits from her internship program, but the real focus would be to see if the two of them could have a real relationship. Barry gave in and the two of them had been together ever since.

Barry felt invigorated by her. He was alive again outside a newsroom. It had been awhile since he felt this way in a relationship. Barry wasn't a rich guy who would attract a girl like Tami normally. And he never fooled himself into thinking it would last forever. *Just enjoy her while you can,* he told himself.

The girl from USC usually didn't try to talk shop with Barry away from the station. Tonight was different. The past couple of days had taken a toll on everyone, and so it was the topic tonight.

"What is the latest on this thing?" Tami asked.

"We still don't have much and you know I can't tell you because it's a personnel issue," Barry reminded her.

"Just tell me the juicy stuff." Sometimes the conversation showed her age. "Is it true that Steve and Jesse were having an affair?"

"Where did you hear that?" Barry wanted to know.

"It's just what everyone in the newsroom is saying," Tami said.

"I don't think they were. In fact, the police can't even put them together that night."

"Why was she found in his bed then?" Tami asked.

"That's the answer everyone wants to find. Let me change the subject. How would you like to learn to run the assignment desk for a few months? It would be a great way to build your resume and learn the inner workings of news coverage."

"Sure." Tami responded with the enthusiasm that Barry loved about her. "What hours do you need me?"

"I need you to take John's hours on the desk from three until noon," Barry said.

"Three in the morning? I hope you're joking." Tami kind of laughed.

"Yes, those are the hours. And, no, I'm not joking. Just until we get through this and I can find a replacement. We'll put you on the payroll and you'll work a full forty hours per week. I really need you to do this for me."

Tami wasn't thrilled at starting her work day so early. She worried it was going to cut into her time with Barry. Right now her hours were very flexible depending on what the news department needed. These new hours would mean she would have to leave their house by 2:30 a.m. She would get home just after noon, and if she was going to make time for Barry, she would have to sleep from the time she got home and the time Barry arrived every night. That was usually around seven or so.

In Barry's mind this was a great schedule. As much as he loved having Tami in his bed, he enjoyed having that big bed to himself when it came to sleeping. Yet another sign of the age difference between the two.

"I'll do it, but only because you asked me to. When do you want me to start?" Tami asked.

"Not tomorrow morning but the next day. I'll make sure there is someone working with you until you get the hang of it."

"That'll be great. Whatever I can do to help you and the station, you know that," Tami reassured her partner.

"Thank you. It means a lot to me that you'll do this," Barry replied.

The rest of the night was dedicated to romance. Barry thought he had forgotten all about romance until Tami came into his life. He forgot what passion was when experienced correctly. Maybe he was falling in love, but he wasn't ready to go down that road. Not yet and not now.

* * *

The Firehouse was a sports bar and tavern where most of the media people gathered after work for a beer or two. On most nights, anywhere from eight to fifteen people showed up. The anchors from the three stations, along with reporters, photographers, and some of the studio staffs would stop by to share in the latest rumors and gossip. The past couple of nights the group from the CBS station didn't show, leaving all the talk about them.

There was a sense of camaraderie among news people regardless of what media they worked for. Steve Johnson, although he didn't hang out after work like the others, was still very well liked. The group really didn't know Jesse Anderson that well because she was so new. The people in the business that met her liked her. The male reporters had taken notice of her the first time she appeared on the air.

Jackson Adams, the NBC anchor, was talking with Phil Roberts, the ABC anchor, when Billie Latzke walked in. It was very rare that three anchors would all show up at the Firehouse on the same night. Billie seldom stopped by, but for some reason tonight everyone was there.

"So, what are you two talking about? Can I guess?" Billie greeted her peers.

Phil was glad to see his sister's friend. They'd know each other a long time. Steve Johnson had been the senior anchor in town. Phil and Billie followed, and finally Jackson, who had only been at NBC three years.

Billie knew what the anchors were discussing and, in fact, you could hear the same discussion throughout the pub. Everyone was telling their favorite Steve Johnson stories. At one point in the night the owner and chief bartender bought the house a round of drinks and everyone lifted a glass to toast Steve Johnson. It was a remarkable moment and it was recognized by each person, even those who didn't know Steve.

"What are you guys going to do to replace Steve?" asked Phil.

"We thought we'd come after you. Isn't your contract about up?"

Phil smiled. He knew Billie was serious.

Jackson interjected for Billie. "I don't have a contract in case anyone wants to know."

Stories and lots of laughter filled the room until 1:30 a.m. and then everyone headed home. It was a good night for the people in the local media and they needed this night. Billie was very happy that she accomplished what she set out to do.

* * *

The morning started early for Barry. He was always up to watch his morning news show. The newsroom thought Barry never slept. He always caught every little mistake no matter when it happened or what show it was in. The only way he could pull this off was by watching every local news show he could. Some news directors ran tape on their shows and then a day or two later played them back. Barry believed in being in the moment. He'd critique it immediately while it was fresh in everybody's mind. That might be another reason why his stations were always the news leader in the market. His track record spoke for itself.

Jake Thompson and Anne Swanson anchored the morning team. Brian Roberts did the weather. The threesome was tightly-knit and had the number one show for local morning shows. The challenge on day three after the bodies were discovered was to try and keep the "no new news" stories fresh. It was impossible without something to talk about. So the team went live from the Johnson house and showed the burnt mattress in the backyard.

Tami was still sleeping when she heard Barry screaming at the TV set. He couldn't believe the morning team didn't know better. Todd, the morning reporter, stood in the backyard and elaborated on the significance of the mattress fire, improvising without a clue.

Two other people were in disbelief as well. Detectives Tracy and Reynolds had started making it a habit to watch the CBS Morning Show to see and hear what they were reporting. Imagine their surprise when they saw a reporter and photographer going live from the backyard of their crime scene.

"Doesn't anyone pay attention to that yellow tape?" Reynolds blurted.

Within minutes of the live shot, Barry called the assignment desk before realizing John was not there. "One day without an assignment editor and stupid shit like this happens," Barry huffed.

Barry called the hotline, a special phone that he had installed at the anchor desk. There were only three people in the station that could use that phone. It was never a good sign when it was ringing.

"Pull the team back in. No more shots from the Johnson house. Understood?" Barry yelled. "I'll be there in twenty minutes."

* * *

On Barry's desk when he arrived at the station were Steve Johnson's phone records. The IT guy was able to get his emails as well as Jesse's sent to his computer. Barry would divide the work up. John would get the phone records from the office phones to check out. He would keep the cell phone records for himself. First he had to meet with his morning team and re-emphasize how their actions were wrong on this morning's live shot. *Wink, wink.*

Barry was thinking about the November viewership ratings that were only weeks away. He needed to figure out who would replace Steve Johnson. When he checked his phone messages on the office phone the only message recorded was from Jackson, the NBC anchor. The time on the message said 2:14 a.m. That told him that Billie had followed through on their plan to put the word out. Barry only hoped the right person got the message. Jackson wasn't that person.

John continued working different sources trying to uncover whatever he could find about Steve's last three hours the night he died. The young reporter wasn't having much luck. John was having a hard time finding anything out about Steve that was out of character for the anchor known in town as the "nice guy." No one had anything bad to say about him. There were no skeletons in his closet. Not a traffic ticket. John decided to focus on the real challenge: how Steve spent his last three hours alive.

Jesse was different in that John couldn't find much of anything about the new girl in town. She seemed to be a loner, although that was hard to confirm because she had only been in town three weeks. Part of his assumption came from the fact that no one at the station knew anything about her. She would work and then apparently disappear. Jesse didn't seem to interact outside the workplace with anyone. The few that spent any time with her at work thought she might be married or have a live-in and that's why she didn't socialize. She was asked to socialize, especially by the guys at the station. But she kept to herself.

An internet geek, John searched different websites, blogs, and water coolers that catered to journalists and couldn't find anything. Maybe he'd find something from her college days. To find that, though, he would need to know where she went to college. John thought Barry would have that information. If nothing else it should be on her resume. When Barry was free, he'd ask him.

The detectives wanted to follow up with Janet Johnson. They placed a call to her attorney, Byron, and now were waiting to hear from him. They weren't very happy with Janet's burning of the bed but there was nothing they could do about that now. The department continued their background checks into the lives of Steve Johnson and Jesse Anderson. They needed to find out everything possible and as quickly as they could. The detectives also wanted to revisit Lisa and Barry to compare notes.

The coroner's office planned to release the bodies. The toxicology report had been reordered to look for poisons, toxins, or anything that might not show up in a regular autopsy. That report should be back later that day. Hopefully, that would shed some light on their investigation and give the police a direction to go in. At this point they still had nothing.

Lisa got to the station around seven thirty and met with Janet before coming to work. Janet had given the station permission to hold a memorial service for Steve so the community could pay its respects. It would be held tomorrow evening at six. There was some talk about doing it at seven, but Lisa was getting pressure from her sales manager and promotion manager that six was best because it would be during their local newscast. Lisa didn't disagree with this thought process, but she didn't want to be the one to bring it up. The public didn't know that these kinds of things happened all the time in local television. No matter how small the TV station, a ratings advantage was still a ratings advantage.

Lisa would take the plans she discussed with Janet and meet with a couple of her station's people to help plan the service. They would do everything they could to keep the service to an hour. Steve's family had arrived the day before from Salt Lake City. His parents were in their seventies and he had two brothers and two sisters that were all married. The station would put together a video of Steve's body of work spanning his eleven years at the station. Lisa would invite a couple of the charities Steve had worked with to say a few words. Barry would speak on behalf of the news room and Lisa would speak as the general manager of the station. The service would be held at the Santa Barbara Mission, one of Steve's favorite places. There would not be a public service for Jesse. Her family was in Texas and didn't seem to want to be too involved with their daughter's remains. Lisa thought it was very sad that she really didn't have anyone that seemed to care about her. The general manager scribbled a note on the pad in front of her to call Jesse's parents to fill them in on the autopsy.

John stood at the entrance to his news director's office waiting for him to look up and acknowledge his presence. "What do you need, John?"

"I'm doing research on Jesse trying to find out everything I can about her. I need to know where she went to college and thought the school might be listed on her resume. Can I look at it? Or can you tell me where she went to school?" John asked his boss.

Barry rolled his chair to his right where there was a set of file drawers. "Here it is. It looks like she got a bachelor's degree in journalism from the Art Institute of Dallas. Make sure you let me know if you turn something up."

"I will, thanks." John started to head back to his desk when he remembered one more question. "Hey, boss. Can I get a copy of the autopsy reports? I want to review them for my research."

Barry was impressed that his rookie reporter was thinking along this line. "I should be able to have a copy for you sometime today."

* * *

Down the street at the police station Tracy and Reynolds were preparing for a second interrogation meeting with Janet Johnson and her attorney. They still had some questions that never got addressed before Janet became overwhelmed with the process and left. Once again, the four people found themselves back in the interrogation room with the tape recorder. Richard turned the machine on and began as he did before the first interview took place.

"This is an interview with Janet Johnson. Present in the room is her attorney Byron Culpepper, police Detective Skip Reynolds, and I am Detective Richard Tracy. It is 8:35 a.m. on October 14.

"Janet, let me say for the record that Detective Reynolds and I are both extremely sorry for your loss." Detective Tracy tried to set a good mood, if that was possible, for this very troubling time for Janet. "Do you know what Steve did after the eleven o'clock news was over the night he died?"

Janet seemed more composed. It might be the fact that she'd had a couple of days to deal with the situation. "I assumed he would just go home when the news was over," she answered the detective.

"Did you talk to him that evening?"

"I talked to Steve around ten o'clock to say good night to him," Janet remembered.

"Did you call him more than once that night?" asked Detective Tracy.

"No, just that one time. I had put the kids down and was going to bed myself when he called," Janet said.

It was Reynolds' turn. "Speaking of your kids, aren't they in school? How is it you were able to take this time to go up to Oregon?"

Byron Culpepper was beginning to think the detectives thought his client was more than just the spouse of the dead person.

"My dad hasn't been doing well and I cleared it with the school. There was no way to leave the kids with Steve because of his work schedule." Janet was starting to get upset again.

"Janet, forgive me for asking some personal questions, but our goal here is to clear you in your husband's death. Can you describe your marriage?" Detective Reynolds was trying to be as gentle as possible, but he really wanted to hear her answer.

"It was good," she stated confidently.

"Then how do you explain Jesse Anderson in your bed?" Detective Reynolds pressed.

"I can't explain it. I don't even know this person. I don't know what she was doing in my bed." Janet was starting to cry. Her attorney reached for the box of Kleenex. "Do you know if my husband had sex with this woman?"

The detectives looked at each other, not sure if they should tell her or not. The attorney asked the question a different way for his client. "Did the autopsy show that the two of them had sex that night?"

"No," stated Detective Reynolds. "There was nothing in either autopsy report that indicated they had sex that night with each other or anyone else."

Janet Johnson was relieved. That question had weighed heavily on her.

The attorney asked, "Then what are we doing here? What motive do you think Janet had to kill either of these people?"

"We didn't say anyone had killed them," Tracy noted.

"Are you saying they weren't murdered? What is going on here?" Now the attorney was the one getting agitated.

"We don't know what happened to Steve Johnson or Jesse Anderson. We don't know how they died. We don't know why Steve was found on the news set or why Jesse was found in the Johnson bed. We don't know." Reynolds' frustration was showing as much as the attorney's.

"We're here because we are hoping that Mrs. Johnson might be able to tell us something that could help us determine what happened that night," Detective Tracy added.

8

BARRY MET DETECTIVE TRACY for lunch. The detective filled his friend in on how the interview went with Janet Johnson.

"You get anything from your background checks on their credit cards or bank accounts?"

"Not a thing. Forensics hasn't turned up anything, either. What do you think the significance of the rope around Steve's neck was about?" Detective Tracy asked.

"You're the detective. What do you think?" Barry shot back.

"It might be symbolic seeing as though the rope didn't have anything to do with his dying. The rope wasn't even tight enough to leave any bruising on his neck." Tracy stated.

Barry was feeling the adrenalin. "It's like none of this makes any sense."

"Maybe that's how it was set up. Maybe none of this makes any sense because it really isn't supposed to." Detective Tracy loved police work because of the challenge a case like this gave him. "Maybe we are overthinking this. Maybe neither one of these deaths are related."

"What are you talking about? How could they not be related?" Barry asked. "She was found in his bed. Of course they're related."

"Forget it. That doesn't make any sense either. We need to find the link between Steve and Jesse."

As the two were wrapping up their lunch, Detective Tracy's cell phone rang. It was his partner calling to tell him that the coroner's office called and the complete autopsy report was ready. He told Barry, and the two agreed to meet at the coroner's office. That would give Barry time to get ahold of Lisa.

* * *

The detectives, Barry, and Lisa arrived at the Chief Medical Examiner's office. No one knew what to expect from the final autopsy report. The news wasn't going to make anybody's day. Tim Samuels was in his fifties and had spent his entire life in Santa Barbara. He became the chief medical examiner seventeen years ago. In all that time he had a total of three unsolved deaths. Once everyone was in the conference room, Samuels handed out copies of the two autopsy reports.

"This is what I will be releasing this afternoon. My findings are inconclusive at this time. I can't determine the cause of death," and then after a pause he added, "to either victim."

"Tim, how can that be?" Barry asked. "No cause of death. That doesn't make any sense."

"I know," Samuels said.

"What did you find? Anything at all that we can work with?"

"Steve Johnson had a little—and I want to emphasize little—heart damage. There aren't any signs that point to anything that might have caused this. The girl, Jesse, didn't have any internal problems that would have killed her. Honest to god, people, I don't know what to tell you."

"Doc, is it possible that they could have been given something that wouldn't show up anywhere?" Detective Reynolds said.

"It's possible but highly unlikely. Most of your poisons are slow acting over time, like rat poison. Rat poison or even antifreeze have been used in very low doses over a period of time to kill people. Almost always we are able to catch something like that in the blood work-up or on close examination of the body. In this case we didn't find anything in the blood work-up, and when we opened up the bodies, neither one showed any signs that you would normally see under those circumstances."

"We're still at square one on this case." Detective Tracy always got his man. He always had evidence, though. "So, Doc, what should we be looking for here?"

The coroner thought before he spoke. "If I were you I would try and figure out the connection between Steve Johnson and Jesse Anderson. The biggest question outside of what killed these two is why Jesse Anderson was in the Johnson bed. Why was Steve Johnson dead on the set? Those two questions seem to hold the key to maybe solving your case. We have no evidence pointing to anything or anyone. I can't even support a suicide theory."

Reynolds held up his arm as if he was asking permission to ask a question. His other hand held the autopsy report for Steve Johnson. "Looking at the Johnson report, it looks like you identified what Steve had in his stomach. Can you tell us when he ate his last meal?"

"Why do you ask?"

"We're trying to close the gap in the time line leading up to his death. We know he got off the air at eleven thirty-five. He was found just before three. Can you tell us if he had something to eat after he got off the air?" Detective Tracy asked.

"It appears looking at the stomach contents that he ate around twelve thirty. It was a pretty good-sized meal. Steak, lobster, salad, and a baked potato, and he washed it down with red wine." The detectives started getting excited. "Alright, now we're getting somewhere," Detective Reynolds said. "There's no way Steve goes home and fixes a dinner like that. We need to find out where he had his last dinner."

"Did you check his credit card records to see if he spent money anywhere, such as a restaurant that night?" Barry asked.

"That was one of the first things we did. He didn't show any activity," Detective Tracy answered.

"What about his neighbors? Did they see anything unusual that night? Did anyone see his car returning home around midnight?" Barry was throwing out anything and everything trying to help.

Detective Tracy tried to answer all of the questions everyone was thinking. "The neighbors said they remember Steve's car pulling in at its normal time. Now, his car was found at the station where his body was found. That means he had to have left his house and gone back to CBS. Nobody remembered seeing him leave, but that would have been probably between one and two in the morning." Detective Tracy looked at Barry. "What would have made him return to the station?"

"Let me get this straight. Doc, you said Steve had a big dinner of steak, lobster, baked potato. Does anyone think he would drive home and fix a dinner like that at midnight? I don't think so. By himself? No way."

"Maybe he left his house to go meet Jesse for dinner," Lisa said.

Detective Tracy added, "We checked out Jesse's place and there were no signs of anything like a big meal. If the two of them had this meal they would have gone out somewhere, and so far we've been unable to turn up anyone who remembers seeing either one of them that night. And besides, what restaurant open at midnight serves steak and lobster?"

Barry nodded. "Did the neighbors say anything about Steve leaving the house once he got there?"

"No one mentioned it, but I'm not sure they were asked, either," Detective Reynolds answered. "Where was Jesse's car found?"

"At the station," said Tracy. "Let's think about this. Jesse's car is found at the station, but she was found in Steve's bed. Steve was found at the station. Is it possible that Jesse rode with Steve from the station to his house? Something happens between the two of them and Jesse ends up dead. Steve drives back to the station and kills himself realizing what he's done."

The coroner wasn't buying any of this. "First, if Steve killed her then how did he do it? Then if he killed himself, again, where is the evidence?"

Lisa was a strong, strategic thinker. It was one of her strengths as a general manager. "What if the two of them had dinner with a third party, not at a restaurant but somewhere else to make sure they weren't seen by anyone?"

"That would make sense and it fits everything we are finding out so far. Doc, was there anything in Jesse's stomach that would tell us she had the same kind of dinner?"

"Absolutely, we would know by her stomach contents. Unfortunately, we don't have the results at this time. We're still waiting on the lab report."

"Doc, how do you classify your findings and this case right now?" Detective Reynolds asked.

"I would call this an unsolved double murder right now."

"Really? You'll go on the record calling this a double murder now?" Barry asked. "What makes it a double murder?"

"Just like clearing the spouse of the crime by process of elimination. I know we don't have a physical weapon at this time. I know we don't have a motive. We have very little evidence at all. At the same time we can rule out accidental death or death by natural causes. That leaves suicide and murder. These two people, according to the interviews of friends and family, would not take their own lives. There is no evidence of suicide on the bodies. No evidence at the locations where we found the bodies. Dead people don't hide evidence. That leaves us with murder. I am confident enough with the lack of everything we have to stipulate now that this is a double murder," stated the medical examiner.

"Will you go on the air and explain this exactly like you just did?" Barry asked.

"I can do that."

"This means there is definitely another person involved. So who do we look for?" Lisa asked.

"I believe you are looking for someone who knows the two of them," the medical examiner said. "By the evidence, or lack of evidence, these killings were not of a brutal nature. That means this person was trusted enough to get close to them. They trusted this person enough to get both of them to meet with him or her after midnight somewhere."

"We still don't know why they would have to meet or why Jesse was in Steve's bed and why Steve was found in the studio," Lisa continued. "And why would Steve have this big, huge meal?"

"It is possible they weren't together. In that case maybe there are two separate murderers," Barry said.

"One murderer, that is all. The person who did this is very smart and meticulous. He or she didn't leave any evidence anywhere. Things were well-planned enough to send confusing messages to the crime scene. I think the only things we know or have found out are the things the killer is okay with us knowing," the medical examiner said.

"The killer must know what this relationship is between Steve and Jesse. Otherwise, why would there be two bodies?" Lisa added. "And if one person outside a two-person relationship knows about it, that means probably some other people know about it. We need to find those people."

***

Several hours had passed. Lisa looked at the clock on the conference room wall. She needed to meet Stewart for drinks at his country club. Barry made arrangements for the coroner to be on the newscast at five and six. He was happy that for the first time in several nights his news team would have something new to report.

9

IT WAS 4:30 WHEN Lisa pulled up outside the country club just a few blocks from Stewart's home. He liked to meet for early cocktails before he went into the dining room. Lisa had a lot to catch Stewart up on, but knowing him he probably already had this news.

Stewart was sitting in his normal, quiet place off in the corner. He liked being against the wall so he could see everyone approaching. He also liked sitting away from people for privacy reasons. Lisa walked over to him, stopping to ask the bar tender if he could put the TV on her station.

"I took the liberty to order your usual drink. Is there anything new on Steve and Jesse?" Stewart asked as soon as Lisa got to the table.

"Well, I just came from the coroner's office. The autopsies are completed and the chief medical examiner is now willing to call this a double homicide.

"That's new. What changed?" Stewart asked.

"In his words, the lack of evidencc of a cause of death. The evidence isn't telling us how they died, and so that makes it all suspicious."

As Lisa was finishing her sentence, a very distinguished-looking gentleman stopped by the table. "Pardon the interruption, but I have to say hi to my favorite person, Masseur Simpson."

"Pierre, the restaurant is wonderful and the food has been superb." Stewart stood up to greet the chef. "Pierre, let me introduce to you Mademoiselle Lisa Campbell."

Lisa extended her hand. "It is truly my pleasure."

"Lisa, this is Pierre Cardeau, our extremely gifted executive chef," Stewart said.

"It is wonderful to meet you, Mr. Cardeau."

"Please, call me Pierre," he said to Lisa. He then turned to Mr. Simpson, "You are too kind."

Pierre Cardeau began to walk away only to turn back to Stewart. "How was the steak and lobster I got you the other night?"

"Perfect. One of the best meals I have ever had," Stewart replied.

"You come in tonight and let me fix you my fantastic chocolate dessert that I know you'll love," Pierre said to the both of them.

"I promise I will be here this evening," Stewart said.

Lisa almost choked on her drink when she heard the chef ask her owner, her lover, her boyfriend, how his steak and lobster was. Was this just a coincidence, or was it possible Stewart Simpson had something to do with Steve Johnson? Or, at the very least, Steve Johnson's last meal. She composed herself so Stewart wouldn't notice, but she knew she had to figure out a way to find out more about Stewart's steak and lobster dinner.

"Steak and lobster?" she asked inquisitively.

"Pierre was nice enough to send over some steaks and lobsters for me the night I got in. It's one of the perks of taking care of people the way I do. Sorry for the interruption. Continue bringing me up to speed. What were you saying about Steve and Jesse?" Stewart acted as if nothing important just happened.

Lisa's mind was spinning. She remembered when she called Stewart to tell him that Steve and Jesse had been found dead. He said he was coming into town that night. That was the first night she met with him on this trip. She couldn't help but think, *What if he had gotten into town the night before? Why though? What could he possibly have going on with Steve Johnson?*

"Lisa, are you out there somewhere?" Stewart's voice startled his general manager out of her thought process.

"Sorry, I was just trying to remember everything I wanted to tell you. The coroner is calling this a double homicide now," Lisa told Stewart.

"That's what you said. Due to a lack of evidence or being unable to determine why either one of these people died." Stewart chuckled at the thought. "That is something I've never seen or heard of before."

"Stewart, there is going to be a memorial service for Steve Johnson tomorrow night. It might be nice if you stopped by. The station employees would be impressed if you did that."

"I might be flying back to Dallas tomorrow morning for a meeting. If I'm here, I will show at the service, but don't count on me."

When Lisa finished her drink she made up an excuse to get back to the station. She knew Stewart would be disappointed that she would not be going back to his place. That was the normal routine, and although it wasn't in the contract, it was certainly understood. Tonight Stewart would just let her go. He wasn't up for the normal course of events tonight. It was better that he let her go back to work.

Lisa's mind kept racing. She remembered telling Stewart about the deaths of Steve and Jesse and how Stewart already knew that Steve was found on the news set—despite not being in Santa Barbara at the time. She remembered he said that people from Santa Barbara called him when they saw it reported on the news. He also knew about "a girl" found in Steve's house—before it was made public. *Curious*, she thought.

On the drive back to the station, Lisa decided she wouldn't share her new information or speculation with anyone until she had something more concrete. It was the only way to protect her owner from becoming part of this investigation. She hoped there would be an easy explanation to everything.

Lisa didn't go back to the station. Instead, she went home. Tom would be there and they could just unwind with an early evening. She often wondered about the possibility of truly loving two men—and cheating on both. There was no real guilt for her. There was a definite sense of concern to keep her husband from ever finding out. Other than that, this was a perfect relationship for her and had been since they married. Lisa knew that most people would not be able to understand the relationship, but she was okay with that. She made sure that she never short-changed Tom in their relationship. Tonight she would let him know that he was the only man in her life. That was all he needed to know.

***

Barry had run the story with the chief medical examiner stating the case was now considered a double homicide. The other news channels didn't have anything on their five o'clock news about it. Everyone had the story for their six o'clock news, but CBS had the actual interview. Not wanting to clap or say anything out loud, Barry was very pleased how the new November rating period was beginning to shape up.

Tami was at Barry's house getting dinner ready. She would start her first day on tomorrow's morning show. Barry thought she had practically moved into his place considering how much time she spent there. Tami, in her mind, had moved in with her boss. Getting up at 2:15 in the morning so her day could start at 3:00 didn't excite her. But being part of this business did. She knew she had to start somewhere. It wasn't lost on her that she was sleeping with her boss. That is not what she meant when she thought to herself she would have to start somewhere. She was in love with Barry but knew Barry wasn't quite feeling the relationship the same way. The age difference bothered him. He knew the relationship would end when Tami got tired of hanging out with the old guy.

Barry's phone rang at the house. His caller ID didn't recognize the number so he almost didn't answer the phone. "Barry, this is Richard. Do you know anything about a second life insurance policy on Steve Johnson?"

"A second life insurance policy?" Barry asked. "I know the station gives every employee a life insurance policy. Who's the second policy's beneficiary? Is it someone other than his family?"

"You could say that. The beneficiary is Stewart Simpson, the owner of your station." Barry could see Tracy smiling a little as he shared this with Barry as if he'd just caught a big break.

"Why would the owner have a policy on our main anchor?

Richard, let me get back to you. I need to check with someone on this. Thanks for the call. Oh, wait a minute. How much was the policy for?"

"A half million dollars."

Barry sat for a period of time thinking about what he just heard. He hoped there was a good explanation but couldn't figure out what it might be. Perhaps Lisa would know about the policy. If she did know, he'd feel a lot better about hearing about it. He dialed his boss's number.

Lisa and Tom had gotten comfortable with a rare night of each other when her phone rang. She didn't have the option not to answer it. Twenty-four hours a day, seven days a week. That was the job description, and she lived it.

"Hello, Lisa speaking."

"Lisa, it's Barry. I just got a call from Detective Tracy. He asked me if I knew anything about a second life insurance policy that had been taken out on Steve Johnson. Second to the one the station gives every employee."

"Okay. I would imagine the family had a life insurance policy," Lisa stated.

"No. This one was for a half million dollars and was taken out by Stewart Simpson."

There was a long pause on the phone. Lisa didn't expect to hear something like this. She wasn't ready to know this. What was she going to do with this information?

"Are you sure about this?"

"That's what I was told by Richard a few minutes ago. In fact, he was calling me to ask me if this was a common thing that owners did on their talent. I told him I didn't know anything about it."

"I'll talk to you tomorrow. Don't talk about this to anyone. Goodnight." Lisa hung up the phone. Instantly, she thought about the chef coming over to the table and asking Stewart about the steak and lobster. How could all of this be a coincidence? She wondered what Stewart would say to her when she asked him about the life insurance policy. So much for Tom getting all her attention tonight, she thought as she walked back to where her husband was sitting.

"Problems?" he asked.

"Nothing out of the ordinary," she lied.

* * *

Lisa woke up fresh from seven hours of sleep. The pill worked. Her first order of business was to call Stewart on her way into the office. She decided she would tell him about the phone call last night. The truth was Lisa wanted to hear Stewart's reaction or what he had to say about the insurance policy. A cup of coffee with Tom and off she'd go.

Barry awoke with a half bottle of wine opened next to him. There were two more bottles of wine next to that one. Tami had gotten up without waking him. Maybe she never got to sleep. He remembered sharing the bottles of wine, making love, and still trying desperately not to think about the detective's phone call. Barry didn't remember much from the evening, so whatever he did must have worked. Unfortunately, he was paying the price for it now.

Lisa and Barry arrived at the station about the same time. She had tried calling her owner a couple of different times but they went straight to voice mail. She thought about asking the business manager if he knew of any such policy the owner had on the anchors. The risk there was if he didn't know about the policy he would now. What if Stewart did this outside the station so no one knew about it?

The phone on the GM's desk was ringing as she opened her office door. "Good morning, this is Lisa."

"Lisa, Stewart. I'm calling to let you know I won't be attending the service tonight." She never thought he would show up. "I'm on the plane heading back to Dallas. I'll let you know when I'm coming back out. Talk to you soon."

Before she could get a word out Stewart was off the phone. He must have known the police were going to want to talk to him. *Another coincidence,* she thought. *There is no way this is not tied together*. Now her boss was on the run to get out of reach of the Santa Barbara police. She had seen this before, but that was a story from a very different time.

Lisa and the rest of the station had a memorial to get ready for. The day had gotten away from all of them. There was still a lot of shock and grief throughout the building. *Murder* was the word being used now. Even with more security added at the station, no one felt any safer. People didn't know if this was a one-time event or if there was a bigger problem involving the station.

John continued trying to figure out what Steve had done his last night. He decided to go to the apartment of Chris Andrews. Chris worked in master control the morning Steve was found in the studio. Master control is commonly known as the department of geeks. It is one of the most important areas of a television station, and yet it is treated as an entry level position. All on-air programming inside a television station goes through master control. That includes commercials, public service announcements, syndication programs, paid programming, all live newscasts, and whatever the network airs.

Chris Andrews worked overnight shifts, which meant he was almost a babysitter. His job consisted of making sure everything aired properly and the commercials all played where they were supposed to. During the overnight shifts there were very few commercials, so the commercial time was filled with public service and station promotions. His real work would start about four in the morning. At five the station brought in a second person in master control because of the morning news show that ran from five to seven. Then there were the news cut-ins for the next couple of hours.

John was struck by the odor of grass coming from outside the apartment. It wasn't heavy enough to catch everyone's attention, but John, just out of college, knew the smell well. He decided to knock on the apartment door knowing this could be embarrassing for Chris. Chris didn't hesitate and answered the door yelling, "Scott, it's about time!"

It was obvious to John that Chris was expecting someone and probably not someone from the station. "Hey, Chris, it's John Rankin from CBS 2."

Chris was shocked and immediately started waving his hand to blow the smoke clear as much as possible. It didn't do much to change the air quality.

"John, what brings you over here?"

"You have a few minutes? I need to ask you a couple of questions about the morning I found Steve in the studio. Would that be okay?" John was still standing outside and hoped Chris would ask him in.

Chris turned and walked back into the one-bedroom apartment. He waved to John to follow. "Sorry about the mess. I've been off for a day and we've been partying a little. So, what do you want to ask me?"

"Did you see Steve come back into the station that night?" John asked his co-worker.

"John, I've already told the police everything I remember. Why are you asking questions?" Chris seemed irritated.

"I'm doing some background work for Barry in the newsroom. We're trying to retrace Steve's last three hours. We know he left the building around eleven forty-five. What we don't know is when he came back to the station," John explained.

"I didn't see anything and he didn't check in at master control when he came back," Chris said.

"Don't we have monitors in master control that show pictures from the security cameras from the parking lot?" John asked.

"We do have security cameras, but the back parking lot camera went out over six months ago. And engineering has never gotten it fixed. Honestly, I didn't see him come back. I didn't see anything," Chris stressed.

John wondered if his co-worker smoked weed on a regular basis and whether he would have really noticed anything out of the ordinary if something had happen. It appeared to him at this time that Chris had probably been loaded from the time he got off work. John remembered something.

"Chris, anyone entering through the back door must punch in an entry code. Is that correct?"

"Yes, they sure do. If the system works correctly there should be a record of every entry."

"Okay, thanks. When do you work next?"

"I have to be back at midnight," Chris answered.

John didn't say anything, but he gave Chris a very concerned look. The two were the same age but they took different paths in their careers. Chris took a job and John had the career. "I would lay off that stuff if you work tonight. The station's crawling with cops."

"John, please don't say anything about the pot. I really need this job."

10

THE SANTA BARBARA MISSION was a beautiful setting for Steve Johnson's memorial service. People started gathering at five fifteen for the six o'clock service. All the local stations and some of the Los Angeles affiliates had live trucks parked around the Mission. Even CNN and FOX News had trucks there. Everyone from the CBS station was at the memorial except for those who had to work, which was most of the newsroom. There were still news shows to do and a good portion would be done live from the service.

The seating area was full and people were filling up the two overflow areas, which had flat-screen television monitors so people would be able to see the service. The Mission estimated that more than a thousand people had turned out to pay their respects. Steve's wife and three girls were as poised as they possibly could be.

Lisa and her husband, Tom, led the station contingency. Barry was there but not with Tami. He still didn't want anyone at the station knowing about his relationship. He scheduled Tami to work the assignment desk during the service. That way the issue of being together was off the table. Tami wanted people to know about them and she made it clear she would gladly leave her job at the station to make that happen. Barry knew that feeling would be temporary for her and she would resent him later if she had to quit her job. He didn't have any doubt that Tami wanted a career in broadcasting.

Detectives Tracy and Reynolds attended together. They were there to pay their respects but to also see if there was someone who caught their eye that they had missed. The detectives were particularly interested in talking to Stewart Simpson, the owner of the station. They didn't know that he had flown back to Dallas that morning.

The casket sat below the makeshift stage. Music played in the background. It was music put together by Steve's daughters. It was their dad's favorite songs. They knew the music well. They've been hearing it all their lives. The three girls enjoyed putting the music together even though they never understood his musical taste. Several photos were displayed around the room of Steve in various poses from his career in Santa Barbara. Local politicians were all present, and when asked they would claim their love and support for the local news anchor. It was now six o'clock and the service began.

"Good afternoon ladies and gentlemen. My name is Josh Stevens and I'm the proud brother of Steve. On behalf of my entire family–Janet, Trisha, Christy, and Dawn, we thank you for your prayers, your support and the love you have shown all of us during this time."

Josh held it together as he made his prepared comments. He seemed as though he had done this before. He hadn't. It was important to him to get this right because of his close relationship with his brother. "Today we choose to celebrate Steve Johnson's life for all the contributions he has made to the people around him. His support of local charities is well known in and around Santa Barbara. Look around and you'll see a community that had great respect for Steve, my brother."

Josh's voice was beginning to break up. After a short pause, to gain control of his emotions, he introduced a list of people who would each take their turn telling Steve stories. Some of the stories were funny and some serious. All had a theme of "Steve Johnson, good guy."

Barry took his turn to talk about Steve as a leader at the station. "As leader in the newsroom, Steve would often fight not to tell a certain story. Or he didn't want to use a person's name, fearing that if that person turned out to be innocent he didn't want to taint their reputation. Yet he was a tough newsman that could go after an interview better than most."

People in the crowd who knew Steve moved their heads up and down as if to agree. "He never met a charity he didn't like. He gave this community his time, his energy, and he loved every minute of his life. Steve was a devoted father and husband. Everyone at the station will miss him."

When Barry finished his remarks, a video started playing on the massive screens placed around the area. The video was a mixture of his news stories showing short clips coupled with home movies that Janet provided.

Lisa would speak next. She had known Steve since he arrived at the station. This was a lot more emotional for her than she thought it was going to be. She had prepared some notes but she wasn't reading from the paper in front of her. "Steve Johnson was my friend. He was my colleague and he was a true champion in local news. I also knew him as someone who loved his family more than anything else."

Lisa had begun to cry. It was more than the service. It was the stress from discovering things about Stewart that she couldn't confirm. "I'm so sorry. I can't continue." Lisa Campbell walked off the stage.

No one in the audience knew what was going through her head. It was a very emotional service and the detectives watched like everyone else who believed this was a general manager who was very close to her employee.

The end of the service came when Steve's three daughters accompanied their mom to the stage. Her voice was soft and almost inaudible. Trisha, the oldest daughter, touched her mother's arm, and then stepped to the microphone. "On behalf of my mother and my two sisters, thank you for being here. It means everything to us."

There was a combined choir made up of children from several local charities that Steve had supported over the years. They sang a few hymns as the service ended and the family exited, followed by the rest of those seated. The burial was to be private the next day.

The Mission at Santa Barbara staged a reception area for everyone to gather. Janet, her daughters, her family, and Steve's family all stayed to thank everyone for coming. As hard as the evening had been, it was a great send-off for one of Santa Barbara's television favorites.

Lisa, Tom, and Barry were standing away from the crowd when the detectives got over to them. "Nice service," Tracy stated. The five exchanged hellos and handshakes. "Lisa, is Stewart here tonight?"

"No, he had some meetings in Dallas and he had to leave this morning. Is there something I can help you with?" Wearing her general manager's hat, she was protecting her owner.

"We'd like to talk to him. Do you know when he's coming back to town?" Tracy asked.

"I can ask him the next time I talk to him."

"We'd appreciate that. Have a nice night, folks." The two detectives walked away to mingle with some of the other people gathering.

Lisa knew the detectives wanted to know about the life insurance policy Stewart held on Steve. She wondered what they would think if they knew about his steak and lobster dinner. Barry hadn't told anyone about this and Lisa wasn't sure she was ever going to tell anyone. Her inner voices were conflicted. *It's just a coincidence. He has steak and lobster all the time and it has nothing to do with this case."*

John saw Barry and walked over to tell him about his conversation with Chris, the kid in master control. He debated whether he should tell his boss or not about the pot and decided it wasn't his place. Barry wasn't happy when John reminded him that the parking lot surveillance camera hadn't been repaired and therefore they didn't have any video of people coming and going. He already knew this because that was one of the first things the police asked for. Barry didn't like being reminded of a missed opportunity.

"Mind if I interrupt?" Barry turned around to see who it was. "Phil Roberts from the ABC station," the person said as a way to remind Barry who he was.

"Yes, Phil, how are you? Let me introduce you to John Rankin, one of my new reporters." Turning to John as the two shook hands, Barry said, "John can you give us a minute, please?"

"Sure. It was nice to meet you, Mr. Roberts." John was close to being embarrassed. He wasn't used to meeting what he considered the top talent in the market. He was still star struck in his own station.

"Please, call me Phil." John started to walk away as Phil said one more thing that would make a huge impression on the rookie reporter, "And kid, you're doing some good work this past week." John couldn't believe that Phil Roberts, one of the top anchors in Santa Barbara, had seen his work. His feet wouldn't touch the ground the rest of the evening.

"Phil, it was nice of you to come tonight. In fact, it was nice to see most of the local news people here tonight. So, what can I do for you?" Barry asked.

"The other night I ran into Billie and she mentioned you might be interested in talking about Steve's replacement. I don't want to do that here because that seems wrong. I saw you standing here and wanted to let you know I would be interested in having the conversation." After a short pause, "When the time is right for you to talk about it," Phil said.

Barry was smiling on the inside. "I'd like that very much. Let's set up a lunch somewhere inconspicuous where we won't have to worry about starting any rumors. Can I get your cell number so I can call to schedule?" Barry took out his cell phone

Phil reached over and took Barry's cell phone out of his hand and began punching in his contact information. "There, now you have my number. I will look forward to talking to you." The two shook hands and walked away from each other as if to try and hide the fact they were just seen together.

Off in the distance Barry noticed Lisa watching the whole encounter. She knew without being told what Barry was up to. It would be a great move and a real steal for CBS to land the anchor from ABC. The news director was always cautious about these types of deals, for many reasons. The main one was because most of the time the anchors from other stations would use these conversations to strengthen their own deal without ever jumping ship. "Let's just see how this plays out," he said under his breath while giving Lisa a thumps up to indicate it was a good conversation.

II

DALLAS WAS A TWO hour time difference but that never bothered Stewart when he wanted to talk. Lisa thought it shouldn't bother him this morning, either. "Stewart, it's Lisa. Say, the Santa Barbara detectives want to talk to you. They wanted me to find out when you were coming back."

"Good morning, Lisa." Stewart thought it was funny how she just jumped into the reason for her call without as much as a good morning. The statement didn't even faze her owner. "What do they want, do you know?"

"Not sure, but I think it has to do with an insurance policy."

"Okay, I'll fly back tonight. Why don't you set up a meeting at the house for tomorrow at ten thirty?" Stewart Simpson baffled his lover sometimes. He always seemed to have everything under control. "Can I see you tonight?"

Lisa thought about her answer. She knew he liked to see her when he liked to see her. The last time they got together she dumped on him and knew he wasn't happy about it. "I can come over around six. Will you be at the house by then?"

"I'll make sure I am," Stewart said, and with that, hung up.

Barry had called a meeting with John Rankin and Carlos

Hernandez to discuss where they were on their investigation. John had kept Barry in the loop daily, but Carlos was doing his own thing.

"So, Carlos, tell us what you've got so far."

Carlos had his pad that he carried for note taking. He flipped through the pages as he began. "I really don't have anything. Usually on a story like this we'll uncover something. It might be a simple little clue that will lead us to a bigger clue, but boss, I can't find anything. There isn't a witness to talk to and the police still have no evidence."

"John, do you have anything?"

"Everything I have I've shared already. Nothing new."

Barry wasn't happy, but he already knew no one had anything. If they did he'd be the first to find out. Barry's sources had come up empty as well. "I'm not sure how to keep this story alive. We've done four days telling our viewers there is nothing new to report."

This wasn't the only investigative team not having any luck. Byron Culpepper, the attorney for Janet Johnson, was on the phone with Johnny, his investigator. "Johnny, how is that possible? You have more connections than anyone I know. Are you telling me that someone might have actually committed the perfect crime?"

"Mr. Culpepper, what I'm telling you is that whoever did this knew what they were doing. They have left no evidence of any sort. No witnesses. Everything I've learned tells me Steve Johnson was a great guy and loved by many. It doesn't appear he was having any kind of sexual affair with the dead girl."

"Then how did she end up in his bed?"

"That's the magic question. If we can answer that, we will probably figure out what this case is all about. The only connection I have found between Janet's husband and this Jesse girl is that he offered to mentor her." The investigator had not uncovered anything.

"What does that mean?" questioned the annoyed attorney.

"Look, this girl was beautiful and just about anyone else would be hitting all over her. Steve wasn't that guy. He is a decent, all-around nice guy. He offered to work with this girl on her story telling and on-air presentation. Steve did all this work at the station and this wasn't anything new for him. He mentored a lot of the new people who came through the station. After checking out every source possible, it appears that Steve Johnson was a very dedicated husband. That's why finding this girl dead in his bed with his wife out of town doesn't make any sense at all."

"Thanks, Johnny. If you think of anything at all that we should try or if you find something out or hear about something, you let me know." The phone call ended.

Lisa was working on getting her own information. The only way Lisa would feel good about it was to eliminate Stewart as a suspect. She dialed the main security gate at Home Ranch Estates where her boss had his house.

"Security supervisor Wilson, please." Lisa waited while the security supervisor was given the phone. "Mr. Wilson, Lisa Campbell, a friend of Mr. Simpson."

"Yes, Mrs. Campbell, what can I do for you?" asked the supervisor.

"I'm trying to retrace my steps this past week for a report I'm doing for Mr. Simpson and I need to know what day he arrived. It was either October 10 or 11. Could you look that up in your records?"

"Not a problem, Mrs. Campbell. Give me two minutes." Wilson went to his computer and looked at his records. "Mrs. Campbell, he arrived on October 9."

Lisa was hoping for the tenth. The ninth put him here in time to have that steak and lobster dinner with Steve Johnson. Lisa hung up and focused on what motive Stewart Simpson would have to murder Steve Johnson and Jesse Anderson. It surely couldn't be the life insurance policy. The half million dollars wouldn't make a dent in his small fortune.

Maybe I should just ask him all these questions and see what he says, she thought. She decided to wait and see his attitude when she met him for dinner.

***

The conference room at the police station was quiet. Detectives Tracy and Reynolds sat at the table, papers scattered, the walls littered with easel pads full of notes. The detectives hadn't turned up a single clue. The second insurance policy was interesting, but it only gave them something to question Stewart Simpson about. Once they knew about the policy, they ran background and financials on Simpson. It turned out that the station owner was solvent, more than solvent. Forbes list solvent. That eliminated the insurance policy as motive. They still wanted to talk to him, but they didn't expect it to go anywhere. Both detectives secretly were looking forward to seeing his house more than anything else.

Lisa hadn't shared what she'd found with anyone else. Not Barry, not the detectives. She debated it over and over in her head. Her loyalty to Stewart Simpson was stronger than her thought of justice, at least for the moment. She probably had the most incriminating evidence of anyone, and it was minimal at best. Despite all the investigations going on separately, and despite the agreement between the police and the station to share information, no one had anything to share.

"Maybe we're looking at this from the wrong viewpoint," Detective Tracy said.

"What do you mean by that?" Detective Reynolds replied. "We've been going at this as if Steve Johnson was the focus of the crime. What if it was Jesse? What if she's the focus and not Steve Johnson?"

"We haven't really focused on the girl because we just never got to her."

"Right, but what if the crime was about her and, for whatever reason, Steve Johnson was accidentally caught in the middle of something?" Detective Reynolds said. "What do we know about this girl?" Tracy was looking through his notes to see what he had. He was surprised at how little they knew about her. He was actually embarrassed at how little detective work had been focused on Jesse Anderson.

"She's from Texas," Reynolds said. "She started at the station three weeks ago as a paid intern after getting her BA degree from the Art Institute of Dallas. Steve Johnson was working with her, more or less, training her."

"How'd she end up in Santa Barbara from Dallas? It's not an easy jump. She doesn't have any family here or any friends." The two detectives had the same thought: They needed to get with Barry Burke.

The two decided not to call but to just go over to the station hoping Barry was there. "Barry, you have a few minutes to grab some coffee?" Detective Tracy asked.

"For you two, I always have time. You want to drink our crap or you want the good stuff?"

"Let's go down the street so we don't have any interruptions," Detective Tracy said. He knew it was impossible to get anything done at the station due to the constant interruptions. The detectives knew that as well. Plus Starbucks was a treat and only minutes from the station.

"Did you guys find something out?" Barry asked.

"Not sure. We want to compare notes with you. What can you tell us about Jesse Anderson?" Detective Reynolds asked.

"There isn't much to tell. I had one of my reporters do a background check on her and we didn't come up with anything out of the ordinary. I hired her about a month ago after she got out of school. Actually, we gave her a paid internship so we could see if she would work out or not."

"Anything else come out of your check into her history? We know she graduated from the Art Institute of Dallas. Did your guy find anything else out?" Reynolds stated.

"There was a rumor he found floating around some of the chatter websites from the school talking about an alleged affair she had with her ethics professor. My reporter, John Rankin, found that online when he was looking into Jesse's background."

"So, why did you hire her if you knew she had an affair with her ethics professor? Especially for news? Doesn't that contradict the character you need in a news person?"

"First, we just found out about an alleged affair. The school didn't appear to take any action as far as we know, and for us, it was a moot point because she's dead and we can't ask her about it."

"How do you think she found CBS in Santa Barbara?"

"She probably did a mass mailing. That is usually how journalism students find their first jobs. They send out resumes and audition DVDs to every news director in the country hoping someone will give them their break." Barry received four or five of these submissions a day.

"Is that what she did?" Detective Reynolds asked.

"Come to think about it, no. I actually got a call recommending Jesse. That very seldom happens, especially from anyone I might listen to."

"Who recommended Jesse Anderson to you?" Reynolds asked.

"Stewart Simpson, the owner of the station." Barry found his words trailing off as he realized what he just told the detectives.

"Did Stewart recommend a lot of news people to you? Why would he recommend Jesse? What do you think the connection is between those two?" Reynolds asked.

Barry now considered his words carefully. He wasn't sure he should implicate the owner of his station more than he already had. "Not very often, but every now and then he might call me up and tell me about some talent he saw."

"But Jesse isn't real talent at this stage of her career. She's a novice. What do you think the connection was?" Detective Tracy pressed.

"I have no idea. They're both from Dallas, so maybe Stewart is a friend of the family. You should probably ask Stewart Simpson that question," Barry suggested. "Here's another question you should make sure you ask him. How come he never mentioned any of this about Jesse Anderson to anyone? He had to know it would be important."

"We will. We're meeting with him tomorrow morning," Tracy said. The statement hit Barry hard because he knew there must be some other reason for them to meet his owner. They had arranged the meeting already. He needed to get to his general manager and let her know what just happened.

12

BARRY WALKED THROUGH the station lobby without talking to anyone. He headed directly to Lisa's office. The door was closed so he knocked. The general manager was meeting with the business manager.

"Lisa, can you give me a few minutes as soon as you're done?"

"Barry, stay. We're done here. I can see you now."

"Lisa, I just had a long conversation with Tracy and Reynolds about Jesse Anderson . . ." He recounted his conversation with the detectives. Lisa gasped at the news. She had no idea that Jesse was recommended for a job by Stewart.

"I should have been informed about this," she huffed.

More ominous was that Stewart Simpson may somehow be involved in the intern's death.

"Barry, I'm sure the detectives will get to the bottom of this when they interview Stewart tomorrow morning. Did they say anything about how they think these two people were killed?" Lisa asked.

"They still don't know. The initial blood work came back, as you know. The full toxicology report takes several weeks. They did indicate that there were covert ways to murder someone by poison, but in almost every case, something turns up in the autopsy. If not in blood work they go to organs, hair, all sorts of tissue. Let's hope this isn't one of those times nothing shows up."

No witness and no murder weapon, Lisa thought. Everything she had heard was circumstantial at best. She wouldn't get much else done today. She would meet Stewart at his Santa Barbara residence around six. Would she tell him everything she knew or just let it unfold tomorrow with the detectives? She wondered if she should ask Stewart about Jesse and what his connection to her might be. It was hard for her to be the jealous one; after all, she once again reminded herself that she was the one in a marriage.

"Lisa, you okay? I thought I lost you there for a minute."

"I'm good. Sorry, I spaced out for a few minutes. Look, I need to get some work done on next year's budget. How's your news budget coming?" Lisa could always use the budget as an excuse this time of year. It was a never-ending project in the fourth quarter.

"The news budget is coming along," Barry lied. "By the way, I'm having lunch in a little bit with Phil Roberts. I want to see if he's got any interest in coming over to our team."

"Good. You know he could play you and use this as a way to jack up his own self-worth at ABC."

"I know," Barry said. "We've seen that before. Either way we win, though. If he gets more money from his owners, that hurts their pocketbook. If we get him on our station, that hurts their ratings."

"And that hurts their pocketbook, too. Let me know what happens."

Barry left Lisa's office not believing the whole budget-work thing. He did get the feeling that she knew a lot more than she was sharing. *Maybe one day she'll fully trust me,* he thought.

***

General Sales Manager David Pedderman thought the week had been a waste. His staff hadn't done anything to put dollars on the books and that infuriated the man responsible for the revenue. He hated missing any opportunity, and that was exactly what he felt happened this past week. Pedderman was sympathetic and he was a team player, though most people thought all he cared about was his next dollar. They weren't wrong, but that is what made Pedderman an excellent general sales manager.

Pedderman had gathered his sales staff to talk about gearing up going forward. Sales people are a funny breed. Everyone inside stations think that sales people are all about having lunches and fun times. Few understood what it took to be a good broadcast sales person. Pedderman had to get his team refocused. CBS was in great shape as a network with primetime shows like *Survivor* and the *CSI* franchises. The station was number one in local news primarily because it had some strong syndication programming with *Oprah, Dr. Phil*, and *Live with Regis*.

Barry swung by the sales bullpen area as the meeting was wrapping up. He wanted to talk to Pedderman and get his take on Phil Roberts anchoring their CBS local news.

"What are you doing to replace Steve on the anchor desk?" Pedderman asked bluntly. "My sales staff needs something they can pitch to advertisers."

"You're heartless, Pedderman, a heartless son of a bitch. We're in the process of looking for Steve's replacement. I'd like to have someone prior to the November sweeps, but that is a pretty quick time table. I don't know that we'll make that one."

"Any prospects you can tell us about?" Pedderman pressed.

"No, and I wouldn't tell you until we actually had an agreement with someone."

Pedderman ended the sales meeting and Barry followed him into his office. He pulled the door shut as he entered. "Uh oh, this looks serious," Pedderman said.

"I'm going to meet Phil Roberts today for lunch. What would you think?"

"I think that would be fucking unbelievable. Do you think you have a real shot at getting Phil?" Pedderman asked.

"You think bringing Phil over to our anchor team would be a good move, then?"

"I think it would be a great move and it would cripple ABC. It's brilliant, and if you pull this off, it will be huge," Pedderman said.

"David, you really think this would be that strong of a deal for us?" Barry wanted to get this right. He knew Pedderman was right about how getting the ABC anchor to move over to CBS would cripple that station. That was a bonus to making this move.

"What do you think we'll have to pay him? Do you have any idea what the anchors across the street are making?" Barry knew he was in the ballpark with what he thought, but he always liked to get someone else's insight.

"I know Phil's co-anchor, Jackie Brown. She's making in the low seventies. Phil's been there longer and is considered their number one man on the news desk. I have to believe he's making close to a hundred," Pedderman said.

Steve Johnson, who was the number one anchor in the market, and had been for eleven years, was the highest paid newsman in Santa Barbara. Steve was making $110,000 and had performance bonuses that could get him to $125,000 if he knocked it out of the park, which he usually did.

"David, keep this between you and me. I'll fill you in after lunch. Keep your fingers crossed." Barry hurried out of the sales manager's office before he got caught up in another conversation that would make him late.

* * *

The drive over to Seafood Grill took twenty minutes. Barry gave himself a little extra drive time in case there was traffic. The Seafood Grill was a little out of the way, which is what Barry wanted for this meeting. He didn't need anyone seeing him with the main anchor of his competitor. Under the circumstances, it would be pretty easy to figure out what this meeting was about.

Phil Roberts arrived right on time. Barry had a table out in the screened-in patio area. No one else was on the patio because of the October air. The cool air didn't bother Barry, but more importantly, he wanted privacy. The two shook hands when Roberts got over to the table.

"Let me say again how classy I thought it was for you and your team to come out to the memorial service. I know Steve's wife really appreciated it."

"Steve and I were friends and he helped me when I came into the market. Plus, he gave a lot to Santa Barbara. It was only right that we recognize that," Roberts said.

"Well, it was very nice." The waitress arrived at the table to give the two news people menus and their water. She recognized Roberts and smiled.

Roberts opened up the real conversation by asking Barry what he was going to do to fill the open anchor chair.

"I'm glad you asked," Barry said with a slight laugh. "That is why we're having lunch. What would you think about jumping over to our station?"

Roberts knew that was why they were meeting today. Ever since Billie dropped the hint at the Firehouse that night he had been thinking about this possibility. "It's got my interest."

"Well, I'm very interested in making this happen. Do you have a contract?"

"My contract is up at the end of the year."

"Have they started talking to you about a new deal?"

"Only in passing, nothing concrete. Our talks will hopefully get serious before the November rating period starts. It would be nice to get it off the table so it's not a distraction."

"You and I both know how this works. By you just having this meeting with me you can now go back to your news director and tell her that I've approached you about coming over. Your stock will go up and you will probably get a better deal. If that is what you want."

"Barry, I appreciate you being so up front. Change isn't anything I like, but working for number one is appealing to me. You're right about the fact I can use this lunch to up my value at ABC. I would like to think that my station would recognize the fact that you might approach me and therefore want to get a deal done with me sooner rather than later."

"You're right," Barry nodded in agreement.

"So, talk to me about the position." Phil wanted to hear the details.

"I'm prepared to make you co-anchor with Billie on all of our main news shows at five, six, and eleven. You would also have the ability to do some major reporting every quarter. Phil Roberts would become the face of the number one local news in Santa Barbara."

Barry was playing to the anchor's ego now. He knew that ABC didn't do much to promote their anchors. He also knew that ABC didn't let their anchors do any reporting. Barry knew that Roberts would love the reporting aspect of the deal.

"What kind of money are we talking about?" Phil asked.

"We're ready to offer you $100,000 a year plus performance bonuses."

The two left the lunch feeling good about each other and the offer. Barry would have to wait for Phil to decide. He told the anchor not to keep him waiting too long. If Phil turned him down, he wanted to be able to move on and find his new person as quickly as possible. Right now, he hoped Phil was that person.

13

LISA WAS UNDERSTANDABLY NERVOUS all day. She couldn't get her boss and lover, Stewart Simpson, out of her head. *What if he's this monster and not the love of my life that I have known the past twenty years? What possible connection does this dead intern have to my seventy-two-year-old boss?*

Lisa didn't know how she was going to approach Stewart. No matter how much she rehearsed her speech, she was afraid she was just going to fall apart when confronting him. And could she really confront her mentor without him feeling betrayed?

Pulling up to Stewart's house, she tried to gather herself as much as possible. Faithful Dugan greeted her as she got out of her car. "Mrs. Campbell, what a pleasure." Lisa instantly wondered what role Dugan played in all of this. She knew he was Stewart's most trusted confidant. There was no chance Stewart was involved without Dugan participating in some way or another.

"Dugan, you're always the charmer." Lisa used this exchange to clear her voice so she could sound as confident as possible. "How's Mr. Simpson feeling tonight?"

"Very chipper. He is really looking forward to seeing you." *Dugan is a good looking man for being in his sixties and still fit as a Marine*, she thought. Lisa couldn't help but guess what Duncan's involvement might be in this whole wretched scheme.

Stewart opened the door just at the right time for Lisa to enter. He had her glass of chardonnay at the ready. They had a light embrace and a kiss before walking into the living room area. The house was always perfectly decorated to fit the time of year. Fresh aromas filled the air. Stewart had Dugan prepare a prime rib for dinner, Lisa's favorite.

There was something odd going on, Lisa sensed. Maybe Stewart had an idea that she was going to confront him about Steve and Jesse. He always seemed to be one or two steps ahead of her and everybody else.

Stewart held Lisa's hand as they walked into the room, leading her over to her favorite spot on the couch. In a way, he signaled for her to sit down. This time, she wasn't in a hurry to kick off her shoes, and she certainly wasn't comfortable. Then Stewart surprised her.

"Lisa, I've got something special for you tonight. I have an early present for you."

Lisa loved Stewart's presents because they were always over the top. "What is it? What's the occasion? It's too early for Christmas."

"I know how hard you've been working and especially how tough this past week has been. I thought I'd give you your year-end bonus a little early. We know how the year is going to end up, so I thought I'd give you something to feel really good about." Stewart reached into his inside coat pocket and pulled out an envelope with Lisa's name on it.

This more than caught her by surprise. *What's going on here? He must know that I have an idea he's involved, possibly with murder.*

She stood up anxiously. "Oh my god, Stewart," her hands were shaking when she opened the seal. Inside was a check made out to her for $125,000, the amount of her annual salary. "Stewart!" she said with a slight scream. "This is four times my average bonus. I know we are having a good year, but not this good. Why so much?"

"I came into some extra money and I felt you deserved this for all your loyalty and hard work the past twenty years. I wanted to give you something special, and I know how much you love your money," Stewart said looking directly into Lisa's tear-filled eyes.

Is this a bribe? Is Stewart buying my silence?

"Stewart, where'd the money come from?" she surprised herself when she heard her ask the question.

Stewart looked at Lisa with the love he'd had for her all his life. There were many, many women throughout the years, but Lisa was the one woman he had loved from the day they met.

"I've never told you this, but I have life insurance policies on all the key people in my organizations. It's something I learned at a very early age. If anything happens and someone dies, someone I've invested a great deal in, then I'm compensated through the life insurance. I protect all my investments, and that includes investing in the people I count on. Our anchors are included in that mix."

Lisa was surprised by Stewart's admission.

"I have the same policy on you as well as your news director, general sales manager, and chief engineer. It is written in everyone's agreement that we contract with."

"I never knew this. I don't remember anyone ever raising the issue and I don't recall seeing this in my contract," Lisa countered.

"It's there," Stewart assured her. "Unfortunately, most people never read the fine print. So, they don't know to ask about it."

Lisa was overwhelmed with Stewart's generosity, and her other thoughts had disappeared as he calmly explained his actions. This gave her a sense of real innocence that she wanted to believe in. She embraced Stewart and passionately parted his lips with her kiss. Money and truth made a strong aphrodisiac. The prime rib could wait. Lisa was going to give Stewart his gift—a night of lovemaking he would remember.

***

The evening flew by and nothing else was said about the investigation or what Lisa had thought. Before leaving, she reminded Stewart that the two detectives would be at his house in the morning.

Lisa drove home that night ecstatic. The bonus would prove to her husband that her years of late meetings and toiling for Stewart had paid off.

Dugan showed Lisa to the door and came back into the residence. "You think she suspects anything?"

"I think being up front with her about the life insurance policy and giving her the bonus helped her get over any of her suspicion. Are you sure the police don't have anything else?" Stewart asked Dugan.

"There is nothing to connect us to any of this except circumstances that you can explain away. This is going to go down as an unsolved case," Dugan reassured his boss. "They have nothing."

* * *

At ten thirty the next morning, the two detectives pulled up to the estate of Stewart Simpson. In all their years on the police department for Santa Barbara, neither one had ever been through the gates at Home Ranch Estates. Dugan met their car and escorted the two into the home. Stewart was in the library. He thought this room gave him a position of authority that would intimidate the detectives. Surely, the common cops would be overwhelmed.

"Gentlemen, it's a pleasure to have you in my home. Stewart Simpson. And you are?" Stewart reached his hand out to shake his visitors' hands.

"Detective Skip Reynolds."

"Detective Richard Tracy."

"Did your parents not like you? What were the chances they'd name you Dick Tracy and you'd turn out to be a detective?"

Reynolds chuckled. Tracy had been there and done that so many times before that it didn't bother him at all. He was impressed that Stewart actually said what he knew others thought and wanted to say.

"Mr. Reynolds and Mr. Tracy, may I offer you a beverage?" Dugan was always the perfect host. "I can get you a water, Coke, or Diet Coke if you'd like. I have wine or something a little harder if you prefer."

Stewart watched the two mull over the offer of a morning cocktail. He was a master at observing behaviors and picking up on anything that might help him be in total control of his situation.

"I'll have a Diet Coke, please," Tracy said.

"Me, too," Reynolds chimed.

"Very well, I'll be right back." Dugan left the room to fetch the beverages.

"I understand you have some questions for me regarding the deaths of my two employees. Please have a seat." Stewart took his seat in the big chair opposite the couch.

Reynolds started as the three took their seats around what appeared to the detectives to be a very old antique table.

"Mr. Simpson, we appreciate you taking time out of your busy schedule to meet with us. We turned up a couple of things that we needed to get some clarification on and they're tied back to you. I hope you don't mind."

Dugan returned to the room with a tray carrying three drinks and three glasses.

"I hope I can be of some help to you. Please ask away."

"Steve Johnson, it turns out, had two life insurance policies through the station. One policy every employee receives, we understand, as part of their company benefits. There was a second policy held by you. You actually got $500,000 when Steve Johnson turned up dead. Can you explain that to us?" Tracy asked.

"It's quite simple, really. I hold life insurance policies on several key employees, including my main news talent, some key department heads, and my general manager. The policy covers my investment in these people. I learned a long time ago that I needed to cover myself in case I lose them. People who are responsible for the profitability of my companies."

"Are the employees aware of this policy?" Tracy asked.

"It's written into their employment agreements. If they read their agreements before they signed them, then they should know. I assume they know about this clause. It's never been an issue."

"What about Jesse Anderson?" Reynolds asked.

"No, I didn't hold a policy on her," Stewart responded.

"She was, no disrespect intended, a low-level employee, as I understand it."

"We know that, sir. We wanted to know what your relationship was with her."

"I didn't have a relationship with Miss Anderson. I only knew her because of this incident." Stewart became stern.

"I thought you recommended to Barry Burke, the news director, that he hire this girl."

"Yes, detective, I did in fact make a recommendation. I don't remember how it came about, but someone I knew asked me if I could give this girl a job to help her career get started. I get job and recommendation requests all the time. You know, I once owned a network of stations around the country, so people always came to me looking for opportunities. I remember making one call to Mr. Burke asking him to take a look at her for an entry-level position. I didn't follow up on it, so I didn't know if he hired her or not. It was only after she was dead did I find that out."

Dugan was just outside the room where he could hear the conversation. He was surprised that the detectives had as much as they did. He hoped they were done with their questioning.

"Mr. Simpson, who was the person that asked you for that favor to hire Miss Anderson?" Reynolds asked.

"I don't remember. It was several months ago," Stewart said.

"Well, if you could remember a name that would be helpful," Detective Reynolds said.

Stewart thought that if they wanted a name he'd get them a name. There were plenty of people that would take this task on for him.

"I'll try and remember. If it comes to me I will give you a call. By the way, have you determined a cause of death?"

"No. The coroner believes a poison of some kind was used in such a way that there was no trace of it found anywhere," Tracy said. "We haven't gotten the full toxicology report back. That will be in a few weeks still. We know that these two deaths were not accidental."

"Mr. Simpson, we really appreciate your time," Reynolds said. "If you could think of the person who asked you to recommend Jesse Anderson to Barry we would like to talk to them. We may have more questions later on. Will you be staying awhile?"

"I come and go a lot due to business. If you need me at any time, I will arrange to be here as quickly as possible. And if I think of the person's name, I will call you. Dugan will show you both out. Thank you again for coming out here to meet me." Stewart stood to make sure the detectives knew the meeting was over.

Dugan, right on cue, came into the room to escort the two men from the library, walking them to the door. As the detectives drove away from the estate they weren't quite sure what to think.

"I don't know, Skip. His explanations seem plausible. I didn't get the feeling he was hiding anything," Richard said to his partner. "We still don't have any real evidence to tie anyone to these murders."

Richard's cell phone rang as they were driving back to the police station. Barry Burke's name popped up on his screen. "Yeah, Barry."

"How'd your meeting go with Mr. Simpson?" he asked.

"We're just now leaving. Nothing really new to report. He answered our questions," Tracy said.

"If you guys have time, why not swing by the station? I'll get Lisa and let's compare all our notes again to see if we have anything new." Lisa was anxious to meet with them to hear what they got from Stewart. She was trying to put all her pieces together without sharing all that she knew.

"We can do that. See you in thirty minutes." Richard hung up the cell phone and told Skip to head to CBS.

***

Stewart and Dugan didn't say much to each other when the detectives left. The two were men of few words, so that wasn't unusual. Their history was over forty years, and by now, Dugan was the closest thing to family Stewart had.

Once Dugan completed the cleanup, he went off to his private suite to retire for the evening. For the most part, he had always lived at the residence. Twenty-two years ago, he lost his wife and son when they were killed by a drunk driver. He practically fell apart, but through Stewart Simpson's intervention got the help he needed to go forward. It was at that time that he moved to the residence, whether in Santa Barbara or in Dallas. Dugan had lost his one love of his life. The rest of his life would be spent serving Stewart Simpson.

Simpson made sure Dugan had privacy by building him a thirty-five-hundred- square-foot wing of his own that connected to the main house. Simpson made sure he kept Dugan safe and without the worries of what people with a normal life would experience. Dugan did the same for Stewart Simpson, but in a much different way.

He retired to his wing of the house and sat down at his computer. From a hiding place known only to him he took out a USB flash drive and plugged it into its port. This was the last thing Dugan did every night before closing his eyes. He proceeded to document the day, his version of a modern day diary. Stewart Simpson would explode if he knew about this.

Dugan learned a long time ago from Stewart that protecting yourself and information was key. He trusted his life to his boss, but he also knew that his knowledge of how Stewart Simpson operated his life and gained his fortune might make him a casualty at some point. He never intended to use this information, but he felt safer having it. Dugan understood the same information would incriminate him as much as Stewart Simpson if it every came out or was discovered.

Dugan wrote in great detail—dates, times, people's names, and a full, detailed commentary that accurately told the stories as he experienced them. Over the years, this file had accumulated stories that fiction writers couldn't even imagine. Names of politicians and business leaders—the crooked ones and not crooked ones—were all listed in chronological order dating back to the 1960s when Dugan first started. He documented an incident in 1975 when he committed his first felony for Stewart Simpson. There would be others.

The early notes were handwritten or typed. Later, when computers became the norm, Dugan spent hours transferring his writings to disc. Through each evolution of technology he would transfer his documents, destroying the original copies. There was only one record and he was the only keeper of the record.

Sometimes he would fantasize what would happen if something unforeseen happened to him. *Would someone other than Stewart find this documentation?* The materials could be used to bribe Stewart or put him away for life. His plan was to destroy these records once his boss died. Dugan thought that Detectives Skip Reynolds and Richard Tracy would be very interested in the writings of October 8 through 10, 2005.

***

The detectives pulled into the television station parking lot and went up to the receptionist, who paged Barry. The news director greeted the two and the trio made their way back to Lisa's office. She didn't want to be in the conference room. Her office was more discrete.

Lisa worried about what she should share, if anything. Should she tell the detectives about the money Stewart had given her last night? It was her year-end bonus. In her mind, she thought it could be hush-money. Her knowledge of the steak and lobster dinner her owner had the same night that Steve Johnson had steak and lobster seemed like evidence and not coincidence. Lisa thought that her twenty-year history with Stewart might become part of this case if the detectives knew more about that part of her life. She might even become a suspect.

"So, what do you two think of Stewart Simpson?" Lisa asked.

"The house is beautiful. Mr. Simpson is a very sharp individual," Tracy said.

"I was surprised at how upfront he was about everything. He seemed very cooperative," Reynolds added. "We asked him about the insurance policy and he explained that this is something he has done with key people that manage or have key roles in his company."

"He mentioned he held insurance policies on the two of you. Did you know that?" Tracy asked.

Barry looked at Lisa a little surprised. Lisa spoke first. "I knew about the policies. They're written in the contracts of key people," Lisa lied. She borrowed a line said to her by Stewart the night before. "I assume that anyone who reads their contract would be aware of this clause."

Barry jumped in, "I have to be honest; I wasn't aware of this clause, but I don't remember ever reading my contract past the money part."

That is exactly what Stewart Simpson counted on when he had his lawyers prepare the employee contracts.

"We asked him about his relationship with Jesse Anderson," Reynolds said. "At first he claimed he didn't know who the girl was until she turned up dead. Then he remembered that someone, he didn't know who, had asked him to help her get her broadcast career started. He said he called you, Barry, and asked you to take a look at her."

"That's right, he did," Barry acknowledged.

"Did he ever follow up on that to see if you hired her or not?" Reynolds asked.

"No, I don't think he ever called me after that first phone call. I'm sure he didn't, or I would have remembered it. It's not like the owner of the station calls me very often."

"That's what he told us. We got the feeling it wasn't any big deal and that because he's the owner he often gets asked to do things like this from friends or such."

"Do you have anything new to share with us?" Tracy asked.

"The life insurance was a surprise to me, but Mr. Simpson's explanation makes sense. I didn't think much when he called me about Jesse Anderson, and he certainly didn't apply any pressure to make me hire her."

Barry didn't believe there was anything new to offer up, but he didn't know what Lisa would add. "My team doesn't have anything you don't already have, I'm afraid."

"It seems like we all have the same information and still nothing to go on," Lisa said. She decided that without the detectives having anything more than what they shared, she didn't need to give them what could be more nothing to consider. She would deposit Stewart's check that afternoon.

14

PHIL ROBERTS WAS HAVING a hard time getting through the days following his lunch with Barry Burke. He kept thinking he should approach his boss and tell her about the CBS opportunity. He didn't want to seem too anxious, but at the same time he was impatient with his own career. Roberts liked everything in order and laid out for him. *Screw patience,* he thought. *I need to know where I'm going to be next year.*

Sharon Miller was petite but had a commanding personality. Outside of putting on a few extra pounds over the years, she was still very attractive. Miller arrived in Santa Barbara five years ago to take over the ABC News Department. She ran a strong news organization. Barry Burke, her counterpart at CBS, thought she had improved their station's look and content enough that he wondered if this was the rating period they would show gains. To Miller's disappointment, the improvement hadn't shown up in the Nielsen rating numbers as fast as she wanted. At least not to the extent that news people in the market thought they would. Miller had been through this before. She knew it took time to change a diary market. Barry knew it too. Getting Roberts to switch stations would extend that time table a little longer.

Nielsen used around 450 diaries over a four-week period to determine what some 500,000 people were watching. Needless to say, change took a long time before it showed up in the ratings.

Miller recognized the knock on her door as that of her main anchor. Roberts entered.

The news director and her anchor had been together a long time. When she got to Santa Barbara, the first thing she did was bring Roberts to anchor her news.

"Phil, come on in and take a seat. What brings you to my office? Miller asked. "I hardly get a chance to talk to you anymore. Everyone's so busy."

"How are you, Sharon?" Roberts asked.

"I'm okay. How about you, Phil?"

"Look, I don't know how to do this other than just come out and say it. My contract is up in ten weeks and I'd like to know what you and the station are thinking."

"Phil, I thought we'd talk about this after the November ratings." News directors always wanted to wait until the next rating book's numbers came out. That usually meant around thirty days after the rating period ended. In Robert's case, that meant not addressing his contract until late December. Using this time table gave the station all the power. If the ratings were good, they were never quite good enough during a contract negotiating year. If the ratings were down, then the station would use that to limit pay.

"Sharon, Barry Burke called me for lunch the other day. He wanted to ask me to come across town," Roberts said.

"What did you tell him?" Miller asked incredulously.

"I told them thank you and I'd have to get back to them. That was the end of it." Roberts didn't tell her that he let Barry know he was interested in talking about this possibility.

"You know you're under contract until December 31? Did they make you an offer?"

"Not really. We didn't talk particulars. I think he just wanted to gauge my interest." Phil didn't want to tip his hand regarding the dollars that were discussed.

"And what's your interest level?"

"I told him that until I knew what we were talking about in terms, it would be hard for me to know how interested I might be," Phil said.

"Did he talk to you about terms?"

"He casually mentioned a number in the ballpark." Roberts sensed his boss's dissatisfaction and that boosted his confidence. He didn't wait for her to ask the obvious question. "Barry told me over six figures plus bonuses."

Miller didn't say anything. She sat there looking at her anchor wondering how she would ever get her general manager to match the CBS offer. Miller knew the answer. The general manager would ask her how she could afford to pay that kind of number when her anchor hadn't delivered the ratings. The ownership had expected some rating improvement the last time they negotiated with Roberts.

It's a fair question, she thought, and as much as she would like to keep him, she wasn't sure she could justify the number without jeopardizing her own job as news director. Her strategy would be to delay doing anything. Her best play was to drag this out and hope CBS wanted the position filled so quickly they would move on to their second choice.

After several minutes passed, she finally responded. "That's a good number. When do you have to let them know?" she asked her anchor.

"I told them I needed to talk to you first. I have a little bit of time, but they do want an answer," Roberts said.

Sharon Miller knew there was an offer on the table. She knew Roberts had a hard time discussing this.

"Okay, Phil. Let me see what I can do. It may take me some time."

"I'm good with that. Just know this isn't anything but a good offer for me. If you want me to stay, the company needs to step up." He got up out of the chair and walked to the closed door. "Sharon, I'd like to stay. We both came here to do something special. I'd like to finish that goal with you."

"Let me see what I can do. I'll get back to you as soon as I know something."

Roberts left her office and Miller sat there in quiet for several more minutes before calling her general manager. His response was as expected. She called Roberts at his desk and asked him to come to her office.

"Phil, come on in." Roberts took a seat. "Phil, I spoke to Don Tippins about your contract. He wanted me to convey to you how important you are to this station and our newsroom."

"That's very nice. Did he put the station's pocketbook behind his words?" Roberts joked. "So where are we, Sharon?"

"Phil, I want you to stay. Everyone wants you to stay."

"And Sharon, I want to stay. But you have to help me make that decision by making me an offer that really tells me you want me to stay."

"We're prepared to offer you a 5 percent increase per year, with a new three-year contract. We also want to make you executive editor of the news. This will give you a title that you'll be able to use from here on out in your career."

"I don't care about any title. I want to know this station values my contributions and pays me what I deserve."

"Phil, in fairness, this contract will put you in the top three of the highest paid anchors in the market. Your ratings still have us as number two in the market. Don and corporate feel this is a very good offer."

"Sharon, I'd be lying if I said I wasn't disappointed. This really is much lower than I thought the station would offer. I told you what CBS was offering me. What do you want me to do with this offer?"

"Honestly, I want you to accept the offer and stay here at ABC. Stay here with me and let's finish what we started."

"If that offer is the best offer you have, then I can't." Phil got up out of his chair and looked Sharon right in the eyes. "This is very disappointing."

"Phil, wait a minute. If you don't accept our offer, then you're done here."

"What does that mean?"

"It means you're through as of right now. If you're telling me that you are not going to accept our offer, then your last day on the air was last night. I will have the business office box up your desk area and we'll get it to you."

"Sharon, I'm still under contract. Did you forget that small detail?"

"No, I didn't forget. Your contract will be honored until the end of the year. You just don't have to come into work. You will be paid through the end of the year. Understand that you cannot work anywhere else until your contract has been fulfilled."

"Sharon, are you serious? You're not going to let me on the air? You're going to pay me not to work?"

"Extremely serious, Phil. If you walk out that door without agreeing to a new contract with us, then you are done as of right now. You can simply go home. We would rather pay you not to be on the air for the next two months and a week than to have you on the air, promoting your presence, just so you can go across the street to CBS. It's up to you. I want you to stay, but you need to agree to a new contract today."

Not believing what he heard, Phil shook his head and walked out the door.

***

Barry Burke was busy at CBS planning out his "sweep pieces." These were the stories the newsroom would create for major rating periods. They were usually along the sensational side. Stations would often sit on reporting important community stories in non-sweep months, if it was possible, just so they could do the story for a ratings month. No one would admit this because that would be against their "journalistic integrity." Those two words made Barry laugh. It wasn't that the words lost their importance to him. It was more that they were thrown around carelessly, and usually by people in the newsroom who hadn't earned the right to be called news people.

He wasn't sure what he wanted to do with the November sweeps. They started in a couple of weeks. Barry knew he couldn't keep dragging out the double murder unless there was a break in the case. Maybe the toxicology report, once it was released, would have something to report about. What about the rest of the time? It was time for one of his brainstorming sessions with his reporters. Barry set the meeting up to happen in two days.

Barry invited his news talent, news producers, Rick Hansen in promotions, and Rick's team. He invited Lisa but knew she was probably too busy to participate. Lisa didn't believe in "sweep pieces." She believed that if you were going to win in local news you needed to do the stories whenever they happened. Barry and Lisa fought about this every rating period. She felt it irresponsible that a news department would sit on a big news story. Yet she understood the financial value of a hot story during sweeps. Barry would argue that the sweep pieces needed more time, needed a graphics touch, and needed promotion. Lisa wondered aloud, "Why don't we approach every day like it's a rating period? Then we would win all the time."

"We do win all the time," Barry responded.

David Pedderman from sales would definitely be at the meeting. Sales wouldn't miss an opportunity to try and get some positive business stories in the mix. Just as important, he wanted to make sure news wasn't going to do anything that might hurt the advertising climate. That happened earlier in the year when the news department decided to go behind the scenes of restaurant health department grades. David and his sales team lost two restaurant advertisers after the station reported their letter grade on the air. He couldn't afford for that to happen again. Revenue, no matter how small, was still revenue.

There were a couple of managers in the station Barry would avoid telling about the meeting. In particular, Doug, the chief engineer, would not be invited. Doug wanted his input heard on every subject. He thought he would be a better news director, a better sales manager, and of course, a better general manager. All everyone else wanted from Doug was his department to fix the equipment and keep it in tip-top shape. Sometimes that was lost on the chief engineer.

The purpose of the news department's brainstorming sessions was to get ideas on the table and see what could be developed. Five ideas would be perfect. One idea a week, starting with the week before the rating period started. That meant Barry and his team didn't have much time for their first story.

One story Barry was working on was an old favorite he had used in every market he'd been in: panhandling. There were people panhandling on a daily basis on busy corners and at stop lights. These people would literally stand in the small islands of left-hand turn lanes in order to ask for money from motorists. Barry had always thought this was very dangerous, that someone could easily be struck by a car. That was one part of the story.

The real story wasn't about traffic safety. This story would be about who these people were and why they did this.

On his route to work, he had noticed the same person, day after day, working one intersection. Sometimes the sign he held up said, "WILL WORK FOR FOOD. GOD BLESS." One sign said, "FAMILY STRANDED. NEED MONEY. PLEASE HELP." Then he saw a third sign. This one had a hand-drawn American flag. "VETERAN HOMELESS. GOD BLESS."

Barry wanted to know his story. How much money did someone like this person make? Why did the Santa Barbara police allow this to occur on a daily basis? Station after station, market after market, it always ended the same.

Barry knew there was more than enough to do a two- or three-part series on the topic. Multiple-part stories were nice during sweeps because they could take up a good portion of the week.

Once Barry explained his idea to the group, everyone jumped on board. Barry was eager to hear more ideas. "Let's move on. Who else has an idea?"

Carlos was quick to jump in. "I'm hearing rumblings about a pyramid scheme starting up and some high-level, local business people are involved. I'd like to look into this and see where it goes."

Pedderman was cautious about this one. "Before we do anything with this one, let's make sure it's a real story first. The last thing we need to do is piss off any of our clients."

Barry was fully aware of the line between news and sales. When Barry started out, there was so much money coming in no one cared if an advertiser got pissed and pulled off the station. There would be a new account to replace it before the commercials stopped. That wasn't the case anymore. Pressure was being put on more and more newsrooms. That's why Barry Burke laughed at those two words, "journalistic integrity." News and sales revenue was no longer separate but tied together, and that jeopardized the newsroom sometimes. That pissed Barry off.

"Look into it, Carlos, and let me know what you come up with. Let's first find out if there is anything to this story." Barry looked around the room. "What else?" he asked.

"What about seeing if we could get inside Oprah's house? Maybe get an actual sit-down interview with her. She lives here now, so maybe she would be open to it."

"That would be big if she would do it," commented Billie, the main anchor. "Do you have anyone you can approach? If you go to her people, they'll tell you no."

"I'm actually working on an inside contact," the intern now on the assignment desk—Barry's lover—answered.

"That would be terrific if you could pull it off. Go ahead and pursue it and let's see where it goes."

The meeting lasted a couple of hours but had to break up so the news team could get their evening shows produced and on the air. Barry was happy with the afternoon's strategy session. He wondered how long it would take before the first person was at his door. As his thought finished, there was a knock. Barry looked up to see his rookie reporter, John Rankin, standing in the doorway.

"I'd like to do the panhandling story." John had learned quickly that the way to get ahead in the newsroom was to be aggressive and passionate. You didn't wait for someone to come to you.

Barry was impressed with the reporter newbie. He liked the aggressiveness that he was displaying. John had done a good job running down some stuff on the Steve and Jesse story.

"John, I'm not sure. It might be too early to turn you out on a story like this. This one is going to take some time and patience to develop. You still don't have any experience." Barry was purposely being tough on John.

"I can do this one. I want to do this one. Let me show you I'm ready."

Those were the words the news director wanted to hear. "Okay, it's yours. Get Carlos to help you on this one. Use Tommy as your cameraman. They both have the experience and can be a great asset to help you. And besides, it was Carlos's idea," Barry reminded John.

John was excited to get the green light but not excited to have to get Carlos involved. He wanted this story all to himself, but he wasn't going to voice his disappointment with his boss.

"Perfect. Thanks, boss." John started to run away.

"Hey," Barry called after his reporter. "I still need you to work on the murder, too. We're going to need follow-up on and we need to be ready in case anything comes out of the full toxicology report."

"Yes, sir. I got it covered for you." John left the doorway and headed back to his desk. Barry was sure he was three inches taller.

Billie walked in, "So, how'd your lunch with Phil go?"

"It was good. Have you talked to him?" Barry was hoping he might have a quick indication as to what Phil might be thinking.

"No, but his sister told me that he has already talked to his news director. That's a good sign." Billie thought it would be great if Phil Roberts came over to CBS. They would work well together, she thought.

***

John, Carlos, and Tommy spent a couple of days mapping out their strategy for the panhandling story. They were beginning to think they were on to something. Barry thought that might happen. He had experienced the same thing in other markets. It was time to fill their news director in and get the go-ahead to take the story to the next level.

"Barry, we think it's time we put a camera on our panhandling subjects." Carlos was as serious as ever. He always tried to display intensity when it came to his investigative pieces. Everyone thought he took himself way too seriously, but Carlos was growing into a pretty good reporter, so the kidding had backed off.

"Subjects, as in more than one?" Barry asked.

"We have three that we know for sure and possibly as many as five," John added.

Carlos referred to his notes. "We've followed the main guy that you turned us on to. He parks his car a couple of blocks from his intersection. We watched him get out his supplies and then walk over to his spot."

"Supplies?" Barry asked.

"He's got his signs, torn clothes, and ragged headband. It looks like it's all part of his costume," Carlos said.

"This sounds like the last time I did this story. So what's the deal with the other people?" Barry asked.

"Not quite sure. We want to put a camera on these people and tail them for a couple of days. Can we get your permission? It might mean some overtime," Carlos said.

John was not happy that Carlos was commanding the conversation.

"Yeah, let's do this. I think you'll be surprised as to what you might turn up. I'll get the team to cover your daily stories."

"Thanks, boss." Carlos, John, and Tommy left the office satisfied that they got what they came for. "Tommy, we need to make sure we do this right and not tip our hand until we're ready to confront them. We're going to need to use your car."

"Why my car? Why not yours?" the chief photographer asked.

"First, because I have a little two-seat sports car and you and the equipment would never fit into it. You, on the other hand, have a van. We can't use the station cars because of the decals," Tommy said.

"Okay, but the station is paying for the gas." Tommy wasn't really upset. He knew this was part of the deal.

"Use my car. I'm so new that no one knows me." John was trying so hard to be a part of the reporting team. He wanted to be taken seriously and he wanted Carlos to respect him. Carlos was making that hard.

Barry earmarked the panhandling story to kick off his sweep pieces. They only had a week to put it together.

The reporters and photographer observed their subject standing in traffic for four hours. It was amazing to them how many people not only gave him money but actually went out of their way to give him money.

"We need to write down a few of the license plates of the people giving money so we can go back to them and ask for a reaction once we break this story," Tommy said.

"That's a great idea." Carlos immediately started writing down license plates. John followed Carlos's lead.

Eleven to one were the high-traffic times on this left turn island. The lunch traffic was heavy due to all the fast food places located after the turn. Another person was back at the location at four and usually worked the island until six thirty or seven.

The third person was part of the original guy's team. There was also a woman involved. She would work the island or the other intersection, depending on where the others were. All four people would meet back at the main guy's car after each stint of collecting. The investigation turned up evidence that showed the main guy would collect the money from the other three.

The first thing they needed to do was run the plate of the car their subject drove to work. Carlos had a contact at the DMV that would check these things for him. It would cost him a dinner and some good inside gossip. The car came back to a William Spencer with an address that was more than forty-five minutes outside of Santa Barbara.

"That isn't where this car is headed," John stated as Carlos shared the information he just got over his cell phone.

"Follow it. Let's see where it goes," Carlos said..

The car drove for about five miles and ended up in a garage storage area. Five to seven minutes passed and the four people pulled out in a new Lexus SUV. The reporters and cameraman almost missed them, except the new SUV pulled right by their car and Tommy recognized the occupants. He yelled to John to follow them.

The Lexus eventually ended up going through a gated community entrance. John had stayed well behind so he wouldn't get detected following their subjects. Once they got to the gate John got right behind.

"This is unbelievable," Tommy said.

"This has to be at least a five or six hundred thousand dollar home," Carlos said.

"What do you want to do?" John asked.

"I think it's time we ask William some questions." Carlos lived for these moments. John was hoping he'd get to ask the questions.

The three piled out of their car as the Lexus pulled into a driveway. The occupants were surprised to see the three people coming up behind them. They were especially surprised because of the camera that was pointed in their direction. "William!" Carlos called.

The driver responded with a quick look as the four people tried to get to the front door as quickly as possible. Carlos persisted, "William, Carlos Hernandez with CBS News. Can we speak to you? We have some questions about your panhandling."

The word panhandling got everyone's attention. "I don't have anything to say," William Spencer answered.

"William, we're going to be doing a story on people who panhandle and we'd like to get your side of the story," Carlos interjected.

"I don't have anything to say. There isn't any story. We're not doing anything illegal," William answered hurriedly. "Now get off my property."

Carlos, John, and Tommy walked back to their car stopped in front of the driveway where the Lexus had pulled in. There was a noise on the side of the house that got their attention. One of the three other individuals had come out the back door and made his way to the side of the house.

"Tommy, go ahead and put your equipment away. I'll be back in a minute," Carlos said.

John quickly touched Carlos's arm. "Let me do this one. It's my story, too."

Carlos was impressed with the young cub reporter's enthusiasm. He thought for a moment and decided to let the newbie take a turn. "Go ahead. But be careful."

John carefully walked over to the side of the house trying to make sure that if someone was watching inside they wouldn't see him.

"Who are you?" he asked as he approached a younger male.

"I'm Chad. Look, Bill can't see me talking to you, but I want to talk. Meet me tomorrow at the Siders Café on Eleventh Street at nine." Chad disappeared to the back of the house.

***

Nine in the morning couldn't come fast enough for John, Carlos, and Tommy. They had never been to the Siders Café. Then again, they hadn't traveled to this neighborhood before. Tommy drove the station van this time and pulled up in front right at 9:00. There was Chad waiting for them. He walked over to the station's van as it pulled into the café parking lot. "We can't stay here," Chad said as he reached to open the side door of the van. He quickly stepped in. "Go. I can't take a chance on being seen."

“Chad, what’s going on here?” Carlos was a little annoyed.

“Bill is pissed that you guys are doing something. He’s been run out of at least two other towns after similar pieces showed up on the local news,” Chad explained.

“So, what can you tell us?” John asked, not bothering to formally introduce Carols or Tommy.

Carlos had a smaller, hand-held camera shooting all the action while Tommy drove.

“Bill found me at a homeless shelter six months ago and offered me a job. He told me I could make some good money to get back on my feet. All I had to do was stand on a corner. He offered me a room and food,” Chad explained.

“So why are you talking to us? It sounds like you have a pretty good set up right now,” John said while noticing how Carlos was doing the best he could to hold his camera steady. It was awkward sitting in the front seat with Chad in the back alongside of John. He hoped the video would be useable.

“Bill is a crook, plain and simple. I was a law student before I had an accident and had to leave school. Then I lost my job and ended up at the shelter. Bill liked me because of my limp. He said it would make us a lot of money. It’s not right, though, and I can’t keep doing this. I’m glad you came along.”

“Chad, we followed you guys to a storage area where you exchanged cars. What is that about?” It seemed to Carlos that John was asking the right questions.

“Bill thought it would be better to have an old beater to drive to our corners so if anyone saw us they would believe our sad stories.” Chad got louder, “Do you know he pays cash for everything? He actually owns that house and the bastard charges us rent. Rent, do you believe that?”

“So you pay for your room?” Carlos asked.

“We pay for our room, the gas to get us to our corners, the food we eat, and a percentage of our corner as well,” Chad continued.

“How much of a percent?” asked Tommy.

“Who are the other two people that were with you yesterday?” Carolos added.

“That’s Sarah and Chester. They have a story like mine. They were down on their luck and Bill found them at different shelters. We all pay Bill.”

"We need to tell this story, Chad. We need to tell your story. You okay with that?" Carlos asked.

Chad was nervous. "I don't know. Bill will kill me. No, it's okay. He needs to be stopped. He takes everyone's pennies, nickels, whatever they will give him."

Carlos, John, and Tommy had their story. It would be better if they could get Bill on camera.

The trio returned to the station to edit the piece shot in the van. They had enough for three parts if Barry would agree to give them that much time. Once it was put together, they showed the piece to Barry.

"You have to get Bill on camera. Get him to say something. Then we'll run the piece. Show the exchange of cars and see if this Chad guy will show you the signs and tell you how they make them." Barry loved the piece.

The three decided to try and get Bill standing on the island. First they would talk to Chad again. John gave Chad a prepaid cell phone that only accepted calls. Chad agreed to take it knowing that John would be the only one calling.

"Chad, we need to meet again. Anyway we can come by the house and talk to you there when William is gone?" John asked.

"Wow, you're trying to get me killed. I can't meet with you again. I gave you too much as it is." Chad was now starting to panic.

"Chad, we need to ask you a few more questions, and if Chester or Sarah want to talk that would be great. Just a few questions, that's all. It's the only way we can get the story done," John said trying to convince Chad.

There was a long pause. It was hard for John, who was so new, so anxious, not to just say something. Then Chad spoke up.

"Okay, but not at the house. Meet me at the storage area at five tonight. William is working the island at that time." Chad finally caved to the idea of another meeting.

"We'll be there." John, Carlos, and Tommy thought of one more part to the story. They wanted to get the city council to comment. They already knew the viewers would be giving the city an earful once these stories ran.

Chad was at the storage facility when Tommy pulled the CBS van up. Chad waved for the van to follow him into a row of garages. About halfway down the garage line there was a double unit with its doors open. Chad signaled them to stop.

Tommy got out of the van first to get his camera set up. Carlos pretended to be on his cell phone in order to give Tommy time. Carlos wanted to capture as much of this on tape as possible. Carlos had the handheld camera as well. John greeted Chad.

"Chad, what do we have here?" asked the reporter when his photographer was ready. "How'd you get the car?" Carlos recognized the old beater as the car they first followed to the storage area a few days ago.

"I dropped everyone off and then had to refurbish our supplies." Chad gave a wave of his hand as if he were Vanna White displaying letters.

Carlos and Tommy were surprised by what was in the garage area next to the old car. John was stunned and could hardly contain the excitement of his first major sweep piece. There was what looked like a couple of dozen old signs and cardboard to make new signs. There was even an art table so they could lay out the cardboard. In the corner was a pile of dirt. "So what's the dirt for?" Carlos was stunned, and he gave Tommy a hand signal to make sure he shot everything.

"That's what we use to dirty up the cardboard so the signs don't look too new," Chad explained.

"Why?" John asked the obvious question.

"William has determined several things that make the difference in getting money from people. New signs don't work as well as old signs. It probably has to do with the attitude that if you're homeless and down, how could you have a new sign?" Chad continued.

"That makes sense. Show us how it's done." Carlos wanted it on camera and he couldn't believe he was going to get it. This would be something else to show William when they met up with him. The plan was to give William one more opportunity to talk.

Chad grabbed a piece of cardboard and placed it on the table. He then opened a drawer and took out one of the black marking pens. He made one of the familiar signs that the three station people had seen on the streets this past week. "Watch this," Chad said as he pulled out what were specially-designed scissors that had rough teeth. "This gives the sign a ragged and torn look." The last thing was to apply the dirt. Tommy was capturing all of it on tape. Chad walked over and grabbed two handfuls of dirt and rubbed it into the sign, spreading it all over.

"This is just one of several tricks that William has taught me. He told me that if I worked at this he would set me up with my own territory." Chad made it sound like they were franchises.

"Territory? What are you talking about? You make it sound as if he has franchises set up," Carlos said.

Chad smiled. "Now you're beginning to see how big this is."

"Seriously, how many territories does William have? And how can he control people from not doing this on their own?" Carlos asked.

"I don't know, but he does. He has people up and down the central coasts all the way up to Monterey. That's a great territory for him because of all the rich people there," Chad stated.

Chad was no longer shy talking about this. *I'm in it this far, I need to tell the whole story now,* he thought to himself. He was no dummy. He was thinking once this story got out he could write a book about it.

"What's this stuff on the wall?" Carlos pointed to Tommy to shoot video of the items on the wall. There were a few hooks that looked like the kind at the end of a pirate's hand. There were several different pants that looked lopsided from one leg to the other.

Chad walked over to the wall and picked up one of the pants and started to slip it on. One pant leg was bigger than the other so the person could fold a leg up inside to make it look like the person only had one leg. Inside the larger pant leg were straps sewed in to make this as easy as possible. Within minutes, Chad looked like a one-legged cripple.

Carlos, John, and Tommy couldn't believe what they were seeing. This story was bigger than Barry even thought. This could be a national story, thought Carlos. 60 Minutes, 48 Hours, or maybe 20/20. All the networks would want this. This could be Carlos's ticket to the big time. John was hoping it would mean a full-time reporter's job for him.

Carlos walked outside and got on the phone. "Barry, we can't go with this story just yet. This is bigger than you ever imagined. You're not going to believe what we've discovered. We're coming back in a few minutes to show you this shit."

Carlos walked back into the garage. "Chad, how much money do you think William is pulling down with his operation?"

Chad thought for a long time. "I don't know. I know he funnels the cash through several different channels so it would be hard to trace it. It's an all-cash business. I know in Santa Barbara we collect sometimes as much as five thousand dollars a week between the four of us."

"And what do you get to keep?" Carlos asked.

"After William takes out our rent, gas money, food, and a business license fee for the corners we work, we keep about 20 percent of our take. Not the group take, but our individual take."

"How does he keep his records?" John asked.

"What records?" Chad laughed. "That's my problem with all this. There are no records. I've kept my own set of records from keeping count of the money I collect and I've determined that he's shorting me close to another 20 to 30 percent."

"What about the others? How do they feel about this?" Carlos had Edward R. Murrow Awards dancing in his head. Maybe a Peabody. News Emmys for sure.

"The others don't ever want to rock the boat. They were truly plucked from being homeless and distraught. They've never had it so good. I know better. I've had better. I was going to be a lawyer. I'm here because of circumstance." Chad was pissed.

15

BARRY BURKE MET HIS news team in the parking lot. The four headed for the first edit bay they could find empty. The raw footage played on the screen with the audio. Barry was stunned.

"I think we've got an organized panhandling operation here that who knows how big it really is." Barry saw something on the screen. "Wait. Roll that video back." Tommy replayed the video. "Hold on a minute."

Barry ran out of the edit bay to his office and straight to a filing cabinet. Inside was a history of his work. He pulled out a beta tape and headed back to the edit bay. "Put this in and play it. Leave your footage on the screen over here"

Tommy did as instructed. "Holy shit!" said Carlos. "It's the same person. This William is in your story as well."

"He's apparently been doing this a long time. Oh my god. This changes everything," Barry said. "You might need more time on this before we blow the lid off it. I want to show this to the Santa Barbara police as well."

The four agreed. Barry would get his detective friends in as soon as possible. Carlos, John, and Tommy would start putting everything together to tell the story so far. Barry thought that this might be a bigger story than the two dead station people. *This is going to be a great November sweeps!* Then came another welcomed surprise: a phone call from Phil Roberts, the ABC anchor.

"Barry, Phil here. Let's do it. Prepare the contract. I'll sign it, and you have a new anchor." Phil was happy with his decision.

"That's great news, Phil. When can you start?"

"Barry, I'm off the air as of last night, but I can't go to work for anyone until January 1."

"Wow, they're not going to use you for the November sweeps?"

"I guess not. It's pretty weird," Roberts said.

"Not really. They probably feel they would be promoting you only for us to take advantage of it when you make the switch. I get it. I wouldn't have done it that way. I would have made you work through the sweeps and then taken you off the air for the month of December. That's just me. I'll draw up the papers."

"Great. Let me know when they're ready to be signed and I'll come by," Phil said.

"Let me ask you something. Would you be willing to do an interview with us? It's news that ABC is dropping their main anchor. It's also news that you'll be coming over here January 1. So let's do a story on it and get your comments. You okay with that?"

"I'm okay with that, but you should check with your attorneys to make sure I wouldn't be violating my contract."

"Good idea, Phil. Let me check with counsel. I'll have Billie do the story herself. She'll call you to set up the interview. This is great stuff, Phil. I'm excited."

"Me to, Barry."

Barry couldn't believe how things were shaping up at CBS for him.

***

Carlos, John, and Tommy were in the edit room when Barry walked in with the two detectives. Barry had laid the ground work for what they were about to see. As the video played, you could see in the detectives' eyes just how amazing this story might be.

"You know we've always turned a blind eye to these guys on the street thinking they were just in bad shape and needed some help," Reynolds said. "We didn't think they ever bothered anyone and figured how much could they really be making?"

"We now have an idea as to how much money they are taking in. We might want to get the FBI and the IRS involved." Richard then added with a chuckle, "I wonder if he has a corner for me?"

"We're running this story next week," Barry said.

"You might have to hold off," Reynolds shot back. "We may need some time so we can round up as much of this syndicate as possible."

"Syndicate?" Barry questioned.

"We really don't know how big this really is yet, but it seems to be well organized. You think Chad would wear a wire for us?"

"I don't know, but I need to run this story," Barry insisted. "This story will air next week. We'll do everything we can to cooperate with you. Hell, I brought you in on this, but I need to run the story."

Barry was concerned that the longer this investigation went on—and now that the local police were involved—a competitor could scoop him on his own story. He knew he wasn't the only one that had police connections. This was his story and he wasn't going to lose it because he sat on it. Barry set out a plan with his team and dispatched them to get William on camera.

* * *

Tommy stood across the street shooting video of the cars coming up to the island where William was working. Carlos walked to the center and stopped. John watched, standing next to Tommy. William recognized the reporter from the other day at his house. He wasn't happy that his work was being interrupted. William took his sign and waved it at him as if to say "go away." He was noticeably disturbed, and then he saw Tommy across the street with the camera.

"William, talk to me. Give us your side," John said to him as he was approaching. John had a second microphone already in his hand. Carlos was chasing after William trying to get across the street. William got to the other side and stopped.

"Ok, what can I do for you guys?"

Carlos was taken by the quick change in behavior.

"William, I'm Carlos Hernandez with CBS Santa Barbara News Channel. We're doing a story on your activities and we'd like your comments. Tommy, show Carlos what we have so far," Carlos said to the cameraman.

Tommy played the complete, unedited version so William would see everything, including the piece with Chad.

"I haven't done anything wrong. The Santa Barbara police have never cited me. So what's the problem?" William responded.

"The problem is you are taking money from innocent people who believe they are helping you," John said. "Your signs say, 'Homeless, need help.' Are you homeless?"

William started walking away. Carlos followed, asking more questions. "William, we have you on video with at least three different signs asking for help. There's 'Homeless, need help.' There's another one that says, 'Vet, hungry, God Bless'. One more reads, 'Stranded need money to fix car.' William, are you a vet? Your car certainly isn't broken. Do you have anything to say to the people of Santa Barbara who you've taken so much from?"

"Tell them thank you. I didn't do anything wrong. I haven't broken any laws." William picked up the pace and disappeared. Carlos, John, and Tommy now had what they needed. The story would air tomorrow night and the next two nights.

Back at the station, Carlos put the finishing touches on his edits and took the complete three-part series to Barry. They showed him what they got from William and what they had for the three-part series.

"There's one more piece to this puzzle," Barry said to his team. "You need to track down some of those motorists and get their reaction. That is part four of your series."

"Good. What about showing this to the city council and getting their reaction? Let's push them to put in place new laws that will prohibit this." Carlos was right and Barry agreed. This story was now a five-part series. A great way to kick off the November sweeps.

"Carlos, one more thing. Stay behind a minute." John and Tommy left the room. "I know it wasn't easy for you to share this story with John."

"Look, Barry. I wasn't happy about this in the beginning. John has something special going on, and the more I was around him, the more I saw the *it* factor. I think John is a keeper. He could be bigger than me," Carlos laughed.

"Just the same. I want you to know how much I appreciate you showing him the ropes on this story. And especially letting him have some air time with you."

* * *

The day was moving very fast. Barry had to excuse himself. The toxicology report was in and Barry and Lisa were meeting the two detectives at the medical examiner's office.

Tim Samuels, the chief medical examiner, was extremely professional and had handled many major murder cases. Most of the time, his findings helped lead the police to a suspect or at least tied a suspect to the crime. Not this time.

Samuels was blunt. "I don't have a lot of new evidence to talk about. We did find some very small traces of sodium azide."

"Sodium azide, doc? Is that what killed these two?" Reynolds asked.

"Maybe. I don't mean to be elusive, but there really isn't enough evidence to pinpoint exactly what killed them. That might also be why whoever did this used a drug like this."

"Where would you get sodium whatever?" Detective Tracy asked.

"Sodium azide," repeated Samuels. "That's the interesting thing. Sodium azide is used for agriculture pest control. It's also used in detonators and other explosives. Here's the real kicker. Sodium azide is used in airbags."

"Airbags?" asked Barry.

"Yes, airbags," Samuels said.

"Tim, how would someone use this drug to kill someone else?" Barry asked.

"The easiest way is to ingest it through food," Samuels said. "It pretty much looks like plain table salt. It also could be ingested through the skin. It's water soluble, but that's unlikely in this case. Sodium azide affects the heart and brain. It doesn't take much to kill someone. Less than fifty milligrams ingested can bring on a comatose state, with a racing heart rate and falling blood pressure. It would take less than five minutes. In water, they would drown before they knew what hit them. Seeing your victims were not drowned, it's most likely they ingested it. A few grams of sodium azide would kill a person in under forty minutes."

"How easy is it to get?" Detective Reynolds asked.

"You can get it if you know about it. This isn't a popular chemical that people really know about," Samuels said.

"At least we have a possible cause of death. Not sure how this is going to help us," Tracy said.

"Tim, can we interview you about your findings?" Barry asked the chief medical examiner.

"Sure." Samuels was never shy about being on camera. He knew it helped his career.

"Are you ready to say that sodium azide was the cause of death?" Barry asked. "Have you determined how Steve and Jesse got this into their system?"

"Again, we found so little of a trace that it is hard to determine, but it's safe to say that in both cases, the sodium azide was ingested by food."

"Finally, something we can work with," Tracy said.

Lisa Campbell sat still, feeling a cold chill and then sweaty as she realized the implication. *Stewart served Steve Johnson dinner the night he died. But why? Why would he do such a thing? Is Stewart really capable of murder?*

* * *

Stewart was coming back into town and Lisa was on her way to see him. She found herself missing him when he was gone. His assistant, Dugan, greeted her by opening her car door. "Mrs. Campbell, you look lovely tonight."

"Thank you, Dugan. How is Mr. Simpson's mood?" Lisa asked.

"He's in good spirits. He's looking forward to seeing you," Dugan smiled.

Lisa walked to the front door where Stewart greeted her with the customary glass of chardonnay. With a light kiss on her cheek and a small hug, Lisa felt relieved and strangely comforted in this odd romance.

"So catch me up on everything. Is there any progress on the killing of our two people?" Stewart seemed very relaxed.

"They've now determined a probable cause of death. It's still undetermined, but the medical examiner says they were killed by a drug called *sodium azide*. Apparently both of them had ingested the drug through food or drink."

"Sodium azide? Isn't that stuff in airbags?" Stewart's knowledge always astounded Lisa. He was certainly one of the brightest people she ever knew, but she never thought about him as being that smart.

"How do you know that?" Lisa asked. "I had never heard of the drug before."

Stewart thought about it for a minute and laughed. "Not sure how I know that. I probably saw it on *Jeopardy*," which was Simpson's favorite TV show.

"Anyway, there is still no direct connection to Steve and Jesse and there are still no suspects," Lisa said.

"Actually, there are connections. The same drug killed both people and both people worked at the television station."

"Yes, but no one can figure out why these two are connected in any way. There doesn't seem to be a relationship between the two. There is no motive, as far as anyone can tell. This case is really nowhere right now," Lisa said.

Stewart refilled the wine as Dugan entered the room to announce dinner. "Tell me about your plans to replace Steve Johnson on the anchor desk." Stewart was always up to speed on every aspect of his station.

"We have an opportunity to get ABC's top anchor. The deal is being finalized as we speak, and we're hoping to announce it tomorrow."

"Sounds like that fell into your lap. Good work," Stewart said.

Dinner lasted several hours and the talk turned away from the station. Stewart talked about his coming trip to Paris and how he wanted her to join him. He was always asking her to go on trips, but Lisa was cognizant of what that would do to Tom, her husband. Stewart knew as well. Lisa thought it was a game that Stewart constantly played trying to make her feel more important in his life than she actually was.

* * *

The next day, Lisa and Barry called Phil Roberts.

"Phil, Lisa Campbell. First off, welcome to the team. I'm excited you're going to be joining our news team."

"Thank you, Mrs. Campbell. I'm excited as well. I just wish I could start work now instead of two months from now."

"Not a problem, Phil. Your start date will be here before you know it. Look, I talked to our attorneys and they thought it shouldn't be a problem with you doing an interview with us. Let's set it up for this afternoon. Barry tells me that Billie will do the interview. You okay with all this?"

"Absolutely, let's do it," Phil said excitedly.

"Great, I'll have Billie coordinate it. Talk to you soon." Lisa hung up the phone and gave Barry a high-five. "Now, let's go over your sweeps plan."

The phone in Lisa's office rang while the two were talking about the November sweeps. The receptionist announced that it was Darryl Smarks, the attorney for William, the person in the panhandling story. "Mr. Smarks, Lisa Campbell. How can I help you?"

Smarks was known for handling sleazy problem clients. "Look, you can't run the story or any of the audio that you have from William on this story."

"The story runs," Lisa said firmly.

"My client will sue you for defamation of character. He will own your station," the lawyer huffed.

"The story runs. Do what you have to do." Lisa hung up the phone and looked at Barry. "You better have gotten this right."

Barry nodded. "No worries here. We nailed this guy."

* * *

That night CBS ran the panhandling story during their five, six, and eleven o'clock news. The second story that night was the announcement that Phil Roberts was leaving the ABC station and joining the CBS station. Across the street, the ABC news director, Sharon Miller, screamed, "FUCK!"

The third story was the CME stating the cause of death in the unsolved murder case. Lisa and Barry were elated.

CBS then ran all three stories again. Twice in their morning two-hour news show and again in both the five and six o'clock evening shows. The station also promoted the entire panhandling series, and the feedback from the viewers was immediate. The Santa Barbara police had warrants prepared and raided William's home as well as the storage garage. William was nowhere to be found. The rest of the group was arrested. Chad was arrested but was released because of his willingness to cooperate and tell the story. The detectives gave CBS the heads-up on their raids, so all of that was captured on camera as well. It was the story that kept on giving.

Every time the station aired the story, they ran a crawl on the bottom of the screen asking anyone who had given to these people to please call a special newsroom number. Carlos and John teamed up to talk to anyone willing to tell their story. The phones rang off the hook. By the next day, the two reporters had more than enough people to talk to. Getting part five done wasn't going to be a problem. They'd already tracked down some of the license plates that they recorded while watching William and his team at work.

***

Lisa watched the newscast from Stewart Simpson's living room. She was proud of everything she saw that night in her newscast but couldn't get rid of the thought that Stewart might be a suspect in the two murders. The nagging thought of his involvement was unbearable, and finally she just blurted out the question she had wanted to ask since she first suspected him.

"Stewart, I can't help but think you know more than you've told anyone about Steve's death. Do you?"

He was surprised it had taken her this long to ask the question.

"Lisa, I won't lie to you. We've known each other too long. Trust me when I tell you, you don't want to know."

"Yes, I do. You owe me that much," Lisa said looking directly into Stewart's eyes.

"I don't owe you anything. I didn't have anything to do with Steve's death. Or the girl's, either."

"What about the steak and lobster dinner? That was the same thing the corner said Steve had in his stomach the night he was killed."

"Yes, I had steak and lobster. I have steak and lobster a lot. I didn't have it with Steve Johnson." Stewart was staying very calm and in control. That was one of his biggest strengths.

"Why the large bonus to me?" asked Lisa with tears welling up in her eyes.

Stewart walked over to her and put his arms around her. He then took his hands and cupped her face, looking directly into her eyes. "I gave you that bonus because I thought you deserved it. Yes, the money came from the policy I had on Steve. I didn't have anything to do with his dying. What? Did you think that I paid you this big bonus so you wouldn't question anything?"

Tears were now flowing. "I did think something like that. I am so sorry. I love you, you know that. I couldn't bear thinking you had anything to do with this. Every time I turned around little things kept pointing at your involvement."

Stewart didn't say anything else but just held her tight. He held her for a long time.

Outside the room Dugan was listening to everything. He was worried Lisa might push Stewart's button and trigger a side that she wouldn't want to see. *So far so good, he thought.*

Once he felt the drama was over, he entered the room to bring more wine for his boss and the one person he felt he shared a kindred spirit with.

Lisa didn't take the refill. She was exhausted and feeling overwhelmed. The drive home would give her time to compose herself enough so Tom wouldn't think anything was up. She kissed Stewart as Dugan brought her car around.

"Mrs. Campbell, drive carefully." Dugan's eyes looked directly into Lisa's as he spoke. He wanted to say something else to her but knew he didn't dare.

16

Dugan had spent the evening as he almost always did, alone in his suite reading or writing. He placed his portable disc into the back of his computer and pulled up his daily writings from October 9 and began reading them to himself.

> *Stewart and I sat down to discuss this girl Jesse Anderson. Jesse was from Dallas and Simpson helped her with her broadcasting career by getting her a job at his station in Santa Barbara. I told Stewart that she was too young and that he shouldn't be getting involved with this girl. Jesse was still in college when they met.*

It was like so many before, Dugan thought, a beautiful twenty-something with a family who really couldn't care less about their little girl. These were the types that Stewart preyed upon. Stewart's relationships didn't really develop past the age of twenty-five. Lisa Campbell was the exception. Stewart loved Lisa and Lisa loved Stewart. They both understood the ground rules. Lisa was married and Stewart had other partners. He continued reading:

I was scheduled to pick Jesse up at two in the afternoon and bring her to the house. Stewart told her that he wanted to talk to her because he didn't like the way things were left the last time they saw each other. That last time was in Dallas before Jesse moved to Santa Barbara.

Stewart and I had planned the day's activities. Steve Johnson would be coming over for dinner after the late news was over. He was told that the owner of the station wanted to thank him personally and talk about a new contract. First we had to deal with Jesse.

Dugan went back to his notes regarding the last visit Jesse made to Stewart in Dallas several weeks earlier. He read the entry into his electronic diary from that day.

September 14, 2005

Jesse Anderson visited Stewart this evening. Stewart thought it was going to be a night of love making, as Jesse would want to thank Stewart for his help getting her the job in Santa Barbara. He had also promised her that he would continue to subsidize her career earnings until she got her career to a place where she could live without his help. Instead, the night took on a different tone. Jesse wasn't there to thank Simpson but to tell him they were over.

Normally, Stewart didn't have an issue when this scene played out with whomever he was with at the time. Tonight was different. Jesse was angry, and she began to threaten Stewart. She told him she was going to go to the police and tell them about their relationship and how he "kept" her like a sex slave. She told him she didn't want anything to do with him ever again, but he needed to keep paying her.

Stewart listened and didn't react until she left the house. Then he went berserk. He couldn't believe that this tramp of a girl who he had taken care of and basically put through college was trying to hold him up. It might be hard to believe, but this had never happened to Stewart Simpson before. He knew his girlfriends could be classified as whores by the outside world. Stewart's world worked for him and his girlfriends.

That night the boss and I talked about what needed to be done. This wasn't the first time we had to eliminate a problem. It was the first time the problem was one of Stewart's sleepovers. Hopefully, Stewart won't want to follow through on our discussion tonight. Only time will tell.

In his next entry he had written:

I picked Jesse up as scheduled. She was off from her new job at Stewart's station. Her mood seemed good and she always got along with me. It was my job to make sure the girls were treated special and to smooth over any misgivings between them and the boss.

Stewart had decided that Jesse was a bigger risk than she was a threat. What the two of us talked about several weeks ago was planned for tonight.

When we got to the house, I escorted Jesse into the living room. Stewart wasn't in the room yet. He was finishing up a phone call in the den. The plan was for me to pour drinks for Stewart and Jesse and to put something in Jesse's drink. I poured a Perrier for Stewart and a diet Coke for Jesse. I dissolved sodium azide in her drink before giving it to her. Sodium azide doesn't have any odor and you don't need much to get the job done. The best part was that it would do what it was supposed to do within a very short time and without leaving much of a trace in her system.

Even writing this doesn't upset me. This was part of my job and I did it without a conscience. Stewart joined Jesse in the living room. The greeting was pleasant. Stewart didn't let on how upset the way they parted had made him feel. He simply engaged Jesse in conversation while she quietly drank her diet Coke. The plan was for Stewart to continue the conversation until such time that Jesse would just drift off to death. Then Stewart had to be Stewart.

Jesse could tell in a very short time that something was happening to her. She knew she felt different and it was obvious to her that Dugan had put something into her drink. She didn't realize how deadly it was until Stewart told her. This was the mean streak that only a few ever saw from Stewart Simpson. Usually this side was saved for business deals and not the girls. I stood outside the room so I could hear what was going on in case anything went wrong. Stewart was careful not to touch Jesse, but he wanted to make sure she knew what was happening and why. He leaned into what was now a limp body and told her that she should never have threatened him. He could never take a chance that a girl like her could possibly try and ruin him. It just wasn't going to happen.

Jesse was gone. Stewart called for me to join him in the room. We picked her up. Stewart had her legs and I took her arms. We carried her to the shower in my suite. We left her there lying on the shower floor to make absolutely sure she had died. Once we were sure, I took her clothes off carefully and, wearing gloves, made sure not to leave any marks on her body. I then turned the water on and let it shower her, making sure not to get any in her mouth so water wouldn't end up in her lungs. Once I was sure any and all evidence was washed away, I dried her off and redressed her. I then placed her in the garage on a plastic sheet.

The plan that Stewart and I conceived had worked perfectly so far. We had nine hours before Steve would be at the house. Steve was told by Stewart not to discuss this meeting with anyone. He wanted this meeting just between the two of them. Steve respected his owner's wishes. It wasn't the first time he was invited to a late night dinner at the owner's house. This had taken place a handful of times during his career, so it didn't feel out of the ordinary when he got this invitation.

I wondered if Stewart hadn't planned something like this a long time ago. He had perfectly set up his male anchor for what was going to happen later this night. Steve would be over around 11:45 after his newscast was over. Stewart watched the newscast.

Steve Johnson drove up to the house. I met his car and escorted him in. I then went out front and drove his car to the garage area. Steve and Stewart were engaged in conversation. Steve seemed very relaxed as Stewart showed him around his house and pointed out some of the special items in his art collection. He was aware that Steve had minored in art appreciation in college.

I called the two to dinner where the soup was already waiting for them when they took their seats at the table. This was followed by the salad and then the main course of steak and lobster. Writing this, it is hard to understand my lack of feeling for what we were doing and what we had already done. Stewart Simpson had been a good teacher over the years. He likened himself to the Godfather, his favorite movie. "It wasn't personal. It was strictly business."

An hour into the meal, Steve Johnson collapsed at the table. I was close by and when I could see he was going out I was there to catch his head. My hands were covered by my gloves to make sure no evidence was found. Once we knew he was expired, we moved him to the garage where Jesse's body was lying.

We carefully placed both bodies in the trunk of Steve's car. My job was to drive Steve's car to his house and pull it into the garage. I had watched Steve drive home several nights to make sure I would not do anything out of his ordinary routine. I followed it to a tee. I made sure to wear his coat and baseball cap he liked to wear so any nosy neighbor would think it was Steve in the car.

I parked the car in the garage. I carried Jesse's body from the trunk to inside the house entering from the garage through the kitchen. I removed her clothes and put her in the bed in the master bedroom. Stewart thought this would be a great distraction, forcing the police to investigate a relationship that didn't exist.

I was surprised at how fast I was able to get this accomplished. My adrenaline was probably the reason. Next I drove Steve's car to the station's back parking lot. I had his electronic pass and was able to use that to get in the back door. The rope was my idea. This was another planned diversion that would occupy everyone's focus for at least a short time, allowing any possible trail to disappear. I threw the rope over the light grid and dropped it down, placing the noose around Steve's neck. At that time of night there was only one employee inside the building. I never worried about the master control operator because I knew he wouldn't be paying attention to anything outside his work space.

Finally, with everything in place, I exited the back door and walked to the street outside the gated parking lot. Stewart was there to pick me up. The two of us drove back to the house. We

> *didn't say much to each other. Once back at the house we made sure anything used was burned in the large fireplace located on my side of the house.*

Dugan finished reading from his writings. He removed the flash drive and put it back in its hiding place. It was the only insurance he had. He hoped he would never need it. In his line of work, you never knew.

17

JOHN RANKIN, THE YOUNG REPORTER, felt fortunate to have had a role in the panhandling scheme story. Although Carlos took the lead, John felt he was very generous about giving the rookie some face time on what could be the story of the year.

But John was equally as frustrated that he had little traction on the Johnson murder case. Now that the panhandling story was completed, he needed to get back on that investigation.

John knocked on Barry's door. The news director knew his cub reporter might be disappointed that he had taken a back seat to Carlos.

"Come in, John. What's going on? Take a seat. You've had a pretty good couple of weeks. You didn't get anything on the two murders, but you did get to work with Carlos and Tommy on the panhandling story. So what's on your mind?"

John was shocked at the bluntness of his boss. He didn't have to say anything because Barry continued without waiting for a reply.

"Look, you're new in this position. You probably thought you were ready, and all I can tell you is that it takes time to develop your skills. What'd you think, that you were going to uncover some incredible evidence in the Steve and Jesse story and solve the case? I gave you the opportunity because of your enthusiasm. It would have been easy to have told you that you don't have the experience. You needed to find that out by trying."

"So why did you let me work on these stories?" John asked.

"How do you think you get experience? Everyone in news has to go through this learning curve. Your learning has just started. Hell, we didn't get it right on the Steve and Jesse story in the beginning. We went on the air saying that Steve's wife was the second victim. It happens. Shit just happens sometimes."

"Barry, I'm not disappointed. In fact, I'm elated about the work I have gotten to do. What I want from you is some of your wisdom. Tell me how I can get better."

Barry remembered what Carlos said about John having the *it* factor.

"Fuck, John. Get up every day and work your ass off. Think out of the box. Practice your craft. Be creative. Work on your delivery. Do whatever it takes," Barry said.

Not quite the speech John was looking for, but he got what his boss was trying to tell him.

"John, you have the makings to be a good reporter. Can you be good enough to make it out of Santa Barbara? That's up to you. But living in Santa Barbara and being a news person here isn't a bad life to live. Hell, only a month ago you were working the assignment desk. Now you're my newest reporter. Get the fuck out of my office and go report something."

John knew Barry was serious and got up and left the office. It was time to go to the Firehouse and join his fellow newscasters.

The Firehouse was filled with news people from all three local stations. There seemed to be a large sales contingency as well. David Pedderman was there entertaining a couple of his sales people. John stopped by their table to say hi. He noticed the sales manager was playing footsies with Carol, one of the station's newest sales people. He noticed this because he had been eyeing Carol from the day she walked into the station. She was John's age and a real knockout.

His first reaction was to try and rescue her from the married sales manager. John had second thoughts and figured he didn't need any more drama this evening.

Pedderman had been married thirteen years and had three

young children. It was easy for him to have a second life outside of his marriage. He justified it by telling himself that as long as his wife never found out it was okay. Pedderman considered himself quite the player, and he usually preyed on the young, new sales girls he hired. He looked at it as part of their training. It was amazing what he could get a girl to do for the promise of one or two big accounts. The girls usually didn't care because they were all single, young, and saw it as a way to get ahead. Occasionally, he ventured outside the sales arena for his encounters.

John was surprised to feel the tap on his shoulder only to turn around and see the sales manager standing behind him. "Mr. Pedderman, sir."

"Call me David. You have a minute to talk?"

John barely knew Pedderman and couldn't imagine what he wanted to talk to him about. "Sure."

"Good. Let's go over there in the corner where we can hear each other. Can I buy you a beer?"

"That would be nice. Thank you," John said.

Pedderman flagged down a waitress and ordered a beer for the young reporter and one for himself. "John, we've never spent any time talking, but I've seen some of your work and you do a good job."

John had no idea where this was going and he started feeling uncomfortable. Pedderman was loose-lipped and slurred his words slightly.

"John, you're working on the Steve and Jesse story, aren't you?"

"Yes, I'm helping out on it. Why?"

"I might have some information for you, but I can't be involved in this. You get my drift?"

"What are your talking about? Do you have some information about the murders?"

"Look, I'm married, but I screw around. I spent some time with Jesse. She told me some things that made me feel like she might be in trouble."

"Mr. Pedderman, you need to tell the police. Especially if you think you might have some information that might help them."

"You're not listening. I can't jeopardize my marriage so I can't get involved. I thought if I shared what Jesse told me, then you could go to the police."

"What did Jesse tell you?" John reached into his coat pocket and pulled out his pen and note paper. "You mind if I take a few notes? It helps me remember key details."

"That's okay. You just can't use my name and I will deny this conversation ever took place." Pedderman took a long drink. "I hooked up with Jesse her first week. She told me that she had been involved with someone who helped her get the job at the station."

"That doesn't sound like a problem," John commented.

"She said this person was holding his influence and money over her and when she told him she was done he flipped out."

"Who is the person?" John asked

"She never revealed his name to me. She just told me that he was a lot older than her and that he had taken care of her and paid for everything she had." Pedderman motioned a waitress for another drink.

"Why would he do that?"

"Sex," Pedderman said rather loudly, annoyed by the question. "She said they had been together a long time, and when she broke it off, she said she threatened to tell people about their relationship. Jesse told me that he became very mad at being threatened."

"You have to tell the police, Mr. Pedderman. What exactly was your involvement with her?"

"Look, I fuck around on my wife. That is what I do. I like fucking strangers. I can't help myself. Whenever a pretty girl gets hired at the station, I make my play. Sometimes, I'm rejected, and more times than not, I score. Jesse was one of the easier ones. She was lonely and horny and wanted company like I did. We were fuck buddies and that's all."

***

John didn't sleep that night. He thought about calling his boss, Barry, but decided he'd wait until morning. He finally fell asleep around 2:30 when the phone rang.

"John, this is David Pedderman."

"Yeah, Mr. Pedderman, everything okay?"

"Look, I was drunk tonight and I don't want you to worry

about anything I said. I don't even remember what I said, but I know I probably talked your ear off. Just forget about it, okay?"

"Not a problem, Mr. Pedderman. Can I go back to sleep now?" John faked being more asleep than he was. "See you tomorrow."

John got up, grabbed a notepad and started writing down everything that had happened. He wanted a clear recollection in the morning. He tried getting back to sleep but couldn't. At seven, John picked up the phone and called his boss.

Barry stirred awake.

"Mr. Burke, can I meet with you?"

Barry recognized the urgency in his young reporter's voice. "What's up, John?"

"I don't want to talk about it over the phone. Can you meet me this morning? It's pretty important."

Barry didn't hesitate. "Let's meet at Denny's for breakfast. It's seven now. How about seven thirty?"

"Thank you. I will see you at Denny's in half an hour."

Thirty minutes later, the young reporter and his boss arrived at Denny's.

"John, you look terrible. You go on a binge last night?" Barry asked.

"I wish that was the case. I have to tell you something, something important."

For the next half hour, Barry listened to his rookie tell him what happened last night with David Pedderman. Barry wasn't showing any emotion as he listened. By the time John was done telling and re-telling his story, he seemed exhausted. The lack of sleep was a big part of it, but so was the emotion that the reporter was feeling.

"Barry, I know I'm on to something here, and I'm not quite sure what to do with it."

"John, I don't know what you have here. I will tell you that I want to call my detective friend and have you tell him what you told me. You okay with that?"

"If that's what you think we should do. What about Mr. Pedderman? He told me to forget about what he told me. What's he going to think if he finds out I not only told you, but that I spoke to the police?"

Barry didn't pull any punches. "Fuck him."

"Barry, I want your promise that I get to tell this story as it unfolds. I don't want you giving this to Carlos or anyone else. This came to me and I want to own this part of the story."

Barry smiled, knowing he had a real reporter in development.

"I will let you do as much of this as you can handle. But, and this is a big but, as soon as I see, or think, that you are in over your head, I will give it to someone else."

"Okay, then. I'll meet with your detective friend. When do you want to do it?" John asked. "And what about Ms. Campbell? Shouldn't we fill in the general manager? I don't want to get fired over this."

"Don't worry, kid. I've got your back."

Barry took his cell phone off the table and punched in Richard Tracy's number. The detective answered after several rings.

"Barry, this better be good. It's eight in the fucking morning and I'm sleeping."

"I need for you to get dressed and come over to Denny's. I have some new information about the Johnson–Anderson murders."

"I'll be there in twenty minutes," shouted back the detective.

"Come alone. You can fill Skip Reynolds in later."

John was impressed at how quickly his boss got things moving. He thought that came from great connections. He wanted to make sure his Rolodex in his cell phone would give him those same capabilities. From this moment on he would make it a point to put every contact in his cell phone no matter how insignificant it might be.

Barry next called Lisa's number. He was relieved when there wasn't an answer. "Lisa, this is Barry. I'm with John Rankin and he's got some information we need to share with our detective friends. Call me when you get this."

Twenty minutes later, the detective entered the restaurant. Barry and John were sitting in the back corner by themselves. They had moved from a regular booth to a more round-table booth so the three would have more room. Richard Tracy slid in.

"So, what's so important that you had to drag me out on a Saturday morning?"

"John here had something happen last night that I think you should know about. Go ahead, John, and fill Detective Tracy in on your story. Tell him exactly what you told me this morning," Barry instructed John.

John had calmed his nerves and wasn't as on edge as he was when he first sat down with his boss. He told the story almost exactly as he did when he told Barry. The detective listened, never touching his coffee. The detectives didn't have David Pedderman on their radar. They certainly didn't know that the sales manager had been banging Jesse Anderson. What else was David Pedderman involved in, he wondered?

After sitting at the table for more than two hours, the three got up to leave.

"What now?" asked Barry.

"I think Detective Reynolds and I need to have a conversation with your sales manager," Tracy said.

John's eyes got big and Barry and Richard noticed. "What's wrong, John?"

"Well, he's going to know that I talked to you."

"That's probably true, but there's no way around it at this point. We have to talk to him," Tracy explained.

"I know, but he's going to kill me," John said.

Barry tried to calm his young reporter. "I'm going to tell Lisa about all this, and she will have to let Pedderman know that you had no choice and that he is not to do anything against you. I told you, I have your back. And John, you can't talk about this or do any story on this until I approve it. Keep doing your homework. Put your notes together. Do whatever you want, but I need to approve anything and everything before we air anything on this. You understand?"

Richard and Barry walked to the detective's car together so they could talk in private. "Look, I don't know what we've got here. It is at least something new to go on. I want to meet with Pedderman today. Can you call him and get him to come down to the television station and we'll meet there in the conference room?" asked Richard Tracy.

"First, I need to get ahold of Lisa and tell her what's going on. She should be the one that calls Pedderman."

"Maybe Lisa should be there as well. That way, you guys can assess what you want to do with your sales manager in case this thing blows up."

"Good idea," Barry said. "Let me reach out to Lisa one more time. Once I talk to her, I'm sure she will want to call Pedderman," Barry said.

"Okay, you do that while I fill Reynolds in."

Barry called Lisa's cell one more time. This time she picked up.

"Lisa, it's Barry." She didn't let on, but she had spent the night with Stewart. Her husband was away on a golf trip.

Barry didn't waste any time getting to the reason he called. Lisa didn't interrupt. He told her the police would be at the station that afternoon to interview Pedderman. She hung up looking pale and shocked. In bed next to her was Stewart.

"What's going on? You look like someone popped your balloon," Stewart said.

"Potential problem at the office involving my sales manager. Sounds like an HR thing. I got to get to the office."

18

LISA AND THE TWO detectives arrived at the same time and walked together into the station. They found Barry, and the four of them walked to Lisa's office. There wasn't much in small talk. Barry gave Lisa an overview of what took place earlier that morning with John Rankin and then with Detective Tracy.

"Lisa, when is David Pedderman due to arrive?" Detective Tracy asked.

"He's due here any time. I told him two o'clock."

Looking at the detectives, Lisa asked them how they wanted to handle everything. "I think we need to bring Mr. Pedderman into the conference room and lay it all out for him. I think we need to confront him about everything we heard," Reynolds said.

"What if he denies all of it? What if he says that John Rankin is a lying son-of-a-bitch and he doesn't have a clue what he's talking about?" Barry was throwing out all kinds of different scenarios when Lisa noticed Pedderman walking down the hall toward her office.

The four got up from their chairs and met the sales manager in the hallway. "Let's go to the conference room where we have a little more room," Barry said as he put his hand on Pedderman's shoulder. He didn't say anything, but everyone could read his nervous expression.

"David, the detectives want to talk to you about some things that came to light this morning. It's got to do with the conversation you had last night with John Rankin," Lisa said.

Pedderman's jaw tightened and his face turned red. He didn't even say anything. He just sat there looking disgusted by the whole scene his careless conversation caused.

"Mr. Pedderman, can I call you David?" Detective Reynolds asked.

Pedderman nodded.

"Great. David, John Rankin told us that you told him last night at the Firehouse that you had slept with Jesse Anderson, the dead girl. Did you tell him that?"

Pedderman looked like someone who wanted to be somewhere else, anywhere else. He was starting to feel ill. Maybe he would get some sympathy if he threw up. *Too easy,* he thought.

"I saw John last night. I honestly don't remember what we talked about." Everyone in the room knew he was lying.

"Well, David, he told us that you were bragging about scoring with Jesse Anderson. Did you say that to him or not?" Detective Reynolds took on a little more investigative tone.

Pedderman looked at Lisa, knowing his job might now be on the line. "What do you want me to tell you?" He held his hands out as if he was looking for some help.

Detective Tracy jumped in. "We want you to tell us the truth. Did you tell John Rankin that you slept with Jesse Anderson? And did you call him around two thirty in the morning and tell him to forget about your drunken ramblings?"

"I don't know what we talked about last night. I had been drinking quite a bit and I might have been bragging to him about sleeping with the new girl. I honestly don't remember. As far as calling him early in the morning, I might have done that. I was pretty drunk and don't remember too much about last night," Pedderman stated.

Pedderman tried not to panic. He thought if he sounded confident and was composed it might go a long way trying to convince everyone he was telling the truth. He was selling it hard, but no one in the room was buying it as the truth.

"Well, let me just ask you the question we all have. Did you sleep with Jesse?" Detective Tracy asked.

"Yes. Regrettably, I slept with her. We hooked up the very first weekend she was here. She seemed lonely and horny."

Lisa and Barry didn't say a word, but each knew what the other was thinking. This might be the end for their sales manager at the CBS station.

"No offense, Mr. Pedderman, but why you?" questioned detective Richard Tracy.

"It was simple. I made myself available and I'm non-threatening to her. I'm married and she liked that I was married because she wasn't looking for a relationship. She really just wanted sex."

Lisa knew exactly what that kind of relationship was about.

"When was the last time you saw her for sex?" Tracy asked.

"We got together a couple of times a week. Most of the time we met during the day. Look, she pursued me. I never chased her. I didn't have to after the first time. She seemed very lonely and she just wanted someone to love her."

The detectives thought there could be more to this relationship and that it wasn't as casual as Pedderman was letting on. They also wondered out loud as to his involvement in her death.

Detective Reynolds never liked guys like David Pedderman, and this was his chance to nail one. "I think you had a relationship with Jesse Anderson and you were passed off quickly because she was so much younger than you. You fell for her hard because you couldn't believe this beautiful girl half your age wanted you. She then rejected you and in a fit of jealous rage you killed her. It happens all the time."

Tracy, Lisa, and Barry were a little shocked at Reynolds' aggressive approach.

"No way, that never happened. We had sex, that was all," Pedderman insisted.

"You can see how this looks. Did she threaten to tell your wife? Is that why you killed her?" Lisa and Barry began to feel sorry for their co-worker.

"I don't know. Jesse didn't talk much about anything. She

told me once that she was going through a bad breakup and she wasn't sure how she was going to handle it. That was the extent of the conversation."

"She never told you who she broke up with? Would you take a polygraph?"

"Absolutely, right now. I just ask that we keep it as quiet as possible. It wouldn't be good for business."

"Or your marriage," blurted Lisa. She was pissed and wanted her sales manager to know it.

Pedderman looked sad as he looked directly at his boss. He knew there was still one more conversation about all this at some point. He wasn't looking forward to it.

"We'll set up the polygraph at the station for tomorrow. We'll keep it quiet. Whether you decide to tell someone or not is up to you," Reynolds said, referring to Pedderman's wife.

Before the meeting broke up Pedderman asked, "Do I need an attorney?"

"I don't know. Do you?" Reynolds snorted as he got up with his partner and walked out the door.

Lisa asked Pedderman to stay behind. He knew what was coming.

"David, I've looked the other way when I knew I shouldn't. You represent this station and this company and you're becoming an embarrassment. I don't know what kind of marriage you have with your wife. Maybe she's okay with how you conduct yourself. The one thing I can't turn away from is when you involve another employee. You know you open us up to a sexual harassment claim. What do you think would happen to us if it got out that you had an affair with Jesse and that you were now being considered a suspect in her murder?" Lisa's voice was stern but calm.

"Lisa, there isn't going to be any sexual harassment charge. I will pass the polygraph tomorrow because I wasn't involved in this."

"David, you admitted to an affair with an intern. Whether or not it was a 'relationship' doesn't matter. I can't ignore these circumstances, nor can I put this station at risk. I am suspending you until we are able to figure all this out. You're not to come to work until I notify you."

"Lisa, come on. I know I shouldn't have had sex with another employee, but it was consensual," Pedderman begged.

"Shit, David. She was an employee and you are a manager. That violates about every workplace rule there is, and it shows very poor judgment. You're not only married, you are a department head, a manager for Christ's sake. An argument could be made that you held your position over her and offered to help her career for the promise of sex."

Pedderman didn't say anything. He hung his head into his hands trying not to cry.

In a caring gesture, Lisa put her hand on her sales manager's arm. "Take your time to compose yourself. Just close the door when you're ready to leave." Lisa walked toward the door, stopping before exiting. "David, take care of you." She didn't wait for a response and headed down the hall to exit the building. Outside in the parking lot, Barry, Skip, and Richard waited for Lisa. "What happened?" Barry asked.

"I had to suspend him until we get this figured out," Lisa said.

"What's to figure out? He had sex with a subordinate. He's a manager and he's an embarrassment to our station," Barry said. The irony that Barry was sleeping with his own paid intern wasn't lost on him.

***

Across town in the private library of Stewart Simpson's residence sat Dugan and his boss. Dugan had copied notes from what the two men had heard from eavesdropping on the meeting in the conference room. Dugan had secretly placed listening devices in several areas at the station he knew Lisa used for important meetings. Stewart, always in control, didn't show any real emotion when Pedderman talked about his affair with Jesse. Dugan knew different. Stewart was jealous; he wanted to be the center of everyone's attention, especially the ladies he literally supported.

"What do you want me to do?" asked Dugan.

Stewart walked over to the tray with a pitcher of water and

a glass on it. Pouring himself a drink, he laid out his strategy. Dugan already knew what to expect.

"This isn't going to be easy to pull off. We already got rid of any evidence that anyone might find, so how are we going to place new evidence for the police to find?"

"The police will find what we want them to find, especially if it's the murder weapon," Simpson huffed.

19

PEDDERMAN MADE UP an excuse to leave the house on Sunday afternoon. That was normally a day he truly put aside for his family. Sunday was his atonement for anything he might have done against his vows during the course of the week. This Sunday would be different. He had to clear his name through a polygraph.

Detectives Tracy and Reynolds spent some time with the person administering the polygraph to make sure he knew what questions they wanted answers for.

David Pedderman arrived at the police station as scheduled at two in the afternoon. He was sweaty and felt light headed. Detective Tracy met him at the counter in the lobby of the station. They politely shook hands, and then the detective walked through the lobby and down the hall where the polygraph room was set up. Before the two detectives left the room, they made sure Pedderman was clear on waiving his rights to have an attorney present. The way Pedderman viewed his actions, they were unethical but not illegal. He had nothing to fear.

The detectives joined Lisa Campbell and Barry Burke in an

adjoining interview room with a mirrored window. They would watch Pedderman being questioned.

The test would take almost forty-five minutes. Pedderman wouldn't know the results until the detectives told him. Outside of showing a certain amount of anxiety, the detectives didn't see or hear anything in their suspect's interview that told them he was involved in anything more than the affair they already knew about. The detectives were smart enough to wait for the confirmation of the polygraph results.

When the polygraph test was over, Pedderman was taken to a holding room while the detectives talked to the examiner. The time seemed to pass so slowly; finally the door opened and in walked Tracy and Reynolds.

"Did I pass?" David Pedderman asked.

"David, the polygraph was inconclusive." Reynolds almost took pleasure in telling his suspect the news.

"What the fuck are you talking about? I had to have passed. I didn't do anything." Pedderman was all but screaming his last words.

"Look, this sometimes happens. But the test didn't clear you. Are you sure you don't have something you want to tell us?" Reynolds asked.

"I didn't have anything to do with Jesse dying. Sex, yes. Murder, no." Pedderman wiped his brow. He was sweating more now than when he was first being wired for the polygraph. "What happens now?"

"You're free to go," and after a small pause, "for now," Reynolds said. "Don't leave the area and make sure you keep yourself available to us in case we have any further questions." The two detectives left the room, leaving Pedderman to consider his situation.

The examiner left the station and headed home. He made his usual stop at the Starbucks where he always stopped for his large latte. Once he had his coffee, he took a few minutes to sit in his normal corner seat. An older gentleman next to him got up to leave as the examiner sat down. There was a paper the elder left on table. The examiner quickly opened it up to find an envelope that he placed in the inside right pocket of his coat. He would deposit the contents of the envelope in his bank.

* * *

Anna Pedderman was waiting for her husband when he arrived home. She'd taken the kids to her parents so she could finally have the heart-to-heart that she had threatened for years. David walked in the door leading from the garage. It was obvious to his wife that he was very distraught, and if history taught her anything with her husband, he would not want to talk about it. This afternoon she promised herself it would be different.

David Pedderman entered through the kitchen to see his wife sitting at the table. He knew he was in for another rough time. For a moment he thought he might be better off back in the lie detector room. "Sit down, David." Anna's voice was soft and yet had a very harsh tone to it. He didn't argue and, in fact, didn't say anything.

"Talk to me, David. You have to let me in. Something is going on and I can't sit outside anymore. Talk to me."

David wiped his hand through his hair. "Everything will be alright. I'm just having a tough time at work." Pedderman had always kept distance between Anna and his work. This was something he did partly because of his extracurricular activities as well as wanting to have privacy in his business life. Something all his own. He was starting to think how much easier this situation would be if only he had shared his work life with his wife.

"Bullshit. What is going on? What happened at work?" David could tell that this conversation was going to be different and Anna was not going to let him off the hook this time. He thought she knew about some of his affairs, but he didn't know for sure. She never pushed him about his whereabouts when he was out late at night. Anna was first a good mother to their three children and that, above anything else, was the most important part of her life. She had all but given up on her spouse being a good husband. In her mind he was only the financial support for her kids. Oh, she still loved him, but she also resented him for how he treated and cheated on her. She knew.

It might have been the stress of the past couple of weeks, or maybe it was the lie detector test, or maybe it was simply the years of lying to the one person who truly loved him. Whatever pushed him over, Pedderman was ready to be honest with his wife for the first time in ten years. He was ready to tell her everything, hoping that she would somehow understand.

For the next three hours, Pedderman poured out his heart, a heart that Anna never knew existed in her husband. He confessed to his multiple affairs. He cried and asked for forgiveness. He told her about Jesse Anderson and what happened over the past four weeks. David didn't leave out any details about anything. It was as if once he started he couldn't shut it off. He even told his wife about what the police had accused him of and about the lie detector test. He hesitated for a moment about whether or not he should tell her about his suspension from work, but there was no turning back now. His wife was either going to stay with him or leave him after this conversation. He decided he was better off putting it all on the table. Anna just sat there and took it all in. She was too numb to feel anything. Her heart had been broken so many times that she wasn't capable of a reaction of any kind.

Pedderman didn't understand his wife's muted reaction. He would rather her scream at him, cuss at him, or even hit him. Her silence was killing him on the inside. Then she did something that was so out of character that it scared him. Anna got up from her chair and walked over to the chest that sat on the living room floor. Without saying a word, she opened the chest and pulled out an object wrapped in a blanket. Her husband watched intently, not knowing what the object was or what she was doing. Anna opened up the blanket to reveal a revolver and a box of ammunition. David's eyes opened wide. He had never seen the gun before and he was afraid what his wife might do.

She walked over to where her husband was sitting and, without a word, she laid the gun in front of him. Her hands held the box of ammunition and she carefully opened it, took one bullet out, and closed the box. David noticed his wife's eyes were dark and lifeless. He knew at the moment that he had destroyed her spirit. Anna took the one bullet and placed it next to the gun. Her message was loud and clear. She picked her purse up on the kitchen counter, and just as David had entered the room, Anna left through the kitchen to the garage. Moments later, Pedderman heard his wife drive away, leaving him by himself with a gun and one bullet.

Pedderman sat at the table contemplating his wife's message. He never picked up the gun because he was afraid he might actually follow through with his wife's wishes. He sat through the night, never getting up from the table and believing his life was truly over.

Several knocks at the door as well as the ringing doorbell startled David. He had barely gotten to his feet when the door popped open with a loud bang. The Santa Barbara Swat Team entered the front room with guns drawn. Seconds later, David Pedderman was on the ground with Detectives Reynolds and Tracy standing over him.

"Get him up. Cuff him. David Pedderman, you're not under arrest. You are being handcuffed for our protection right now."

"Gun on the table," shouted Tracy to his partner.

"David, what's the story with the gun? Were you thinking about suicide?" Tracy asked.

David didn't answer. He was in shock over what had just happened in a matter of seconds. "What is going on, detectives? Tell me something." His voice was cracking under the pressure of the past twelve hours. "What is this about?"

"Mr. Pedderman, we have a search warrant for your residence, your car, and your office." Reynolds placed the paperwork in his cuffed hands. "If you have anything in the house or garage that we're going to find, you'd be doing everyone a favor by telling us now."

"Detective Reynolds, I don't know what you are talking about. What are you looking for?"

"Have a seat." Reynolds guided his suspect down on to the chair. Tracy was going through the kitchen cupboards. Reynolds started in the dining room and living room. The house was full of officers going through every drawer, looking under cushions, and between the mattresses in every bedroom. "David, where is your wife?"

Pedderman looked up with tears in his eyes. "She left me."

"Skip, come out here, will you?" Tracy called, standing in the doorway leading to the garage. There was an officer standing in the garage over a barrel that was tucked away under a shelf and covered by a blanket.

"What did you find?" Reynolds asked.

"Take a look. There's what appears to be an air bag that is all cut up in a plastic bag. Didn't the medical examiner tell us that the poison he suspected in the murders was a chemical used in airbags?"

"Yes, he did." Reynolds took the plastic bag from his partner's hand and walked it into the living room where his now-murder suspect was sitting.

"Mr. Pedderman, do you know what this is?"

"Trash?" he questioned. Trying to figure out what was in the plastic bag held in front of him he quietly stated, "I have no idea."

"If I'm not mistaken, it is a cut-up air bag from a car," Reynolds said.

"Now, why would you have this hidden away in your garage?" asked Tracy.

Pedderman had a lost expression on his face. He thought he clearly was losing his mind. "I've never seen that before." Moments of silence followed before he asked the detectives, "And why does it matter? It looks like trash."

"David, the medical examiner believes the chemical sodium azide was used to kill Jesse Anderson and Steve Johnson," Reynolds said.

"So?"

"Sodium azide is found in airbags." Detective Tracy was now taking the lead in the conversation.

The police officer that found the plastic bag containing the air bag waived to Tracy to come over to him in the kitchen. They talked for a minute before the detective returned to his partner and their suspect in the living room.

The search in the rest of the house didn't turn up anything. The two detectives conferred several times and then decided they still didn't have enough to hold the sales manager for murder. They certainly were getting closer, but until they got a lab report back from forensics, they didn't feel they had enough to charge Pedderman. They hoped the lab would confirm the hidden plastic bag was possibly the murder weapon. They also decided against putting him in protective custody. He didn't appear to be suicidal, despite the gun.

20

DUGAN HUNG UP THE phone and walked into the library where Stewart Simpson was sitting. “Everything is in place, sir. The rest will be taken care of tonight. Would you like your breakfast, now?”

“Please. Let me have two pieces of whole wheat toast, dry, with two boiled eggs. Anything I need to know about how this will be done?” Stewart asked the question that he didn’t really want an answer to.

“No, sir. It’s all being handled with very capable contract labor.”

* * *

Barry got a call from Detective Tracy, who filled him in on the Monday morning raid on David Pedderman’s home. He told him everything. Even about the gun found on the table with one bullet next to it. The two men speculated that the station’s sales manager was probably thinking of suicide, believing he was about to be caught for the two murders but that he didn’t have the nerve to go through with it.

After hanging up the phone, Barry went down the hall to see his general manager. Lisa was thumbing through papers on her desk when Barry knocked on the door and walked in. He filled her in on his conversation with Detective Tracy. The two TV executives were in somewhat of a shock. They had known David Pedderman a long time, and even though they both thought he was a "sleazy salesman" who fucked around with anyone he could, they never thought he was capable of murder.

Lisa felt relieved in one way. *At least it wasn't Stewart.* She was heartsick over her sales manager, but thankful that her boss and lover was not involved.

* * *

John Rankin met Barry as he was going back into his office. "Come on in, John. What's up?"

"I know about the raid on Pedderman's house. I know about the trash bag that was found with the air bag. And I know about the chemical that is being thought of as the murder weapon, which is used in airbags. I want to run with this story on the news tonight."

The news director was seeing his young reporter grow up before his eyes. He was impressed that this young kid had already gotten his own inside sources and that the information was accurate.

"You can do the story, but not yet. Besides, no arrest has been made. You can't name Pedderman as a suspect until the police make it official."

John suspected that his boss might be sitting on a story simply because it involved one of their own. "Mr. Burke, we can't ignore this story because it involves someone who works here."

"We're not ignoring it. I just want you to hold off until an arrest is officially made. You'll still beat the competition because we'll know as soon as Pedderman is picked up, if that indeed happens. Besides, I want to give Lisa some time to figure out how she is going to handle this from a PR standpoint." Barry took a couple of breaths before he continued. "So, who's your source on the inside?"

"You know I can't tell you," John said.

"Can't? Or won't?" Barry asked.

"Either one, I'm not telling you." John walked out of Barry's office. The kid wasn't about to let this one go. He thought about calling the sales manager, ostensibly to see if he was okay. What he truly wanted was to see was if Pedderman would talk to him. It did worry him that Pedderman might be pissed that he was the one that told about their conversation and that's what started this whole downturn. Maybe he would just drive over and see him in person. The truth was he'd like to talk to Pedderman on camera before the police arrested him. Everyone at the station speculated his arrest was going to happen—and soon.

Local broadcasting was the worst when it came to rumors, speculation, and just plain lies. This was especially true when it came to lies about co-workers or their peers at other stations. It didn't seem to matter if it was a station in Los Angeles or New York or a station in Santa Barbara. Broadcast people in general loved to gossip and slam people, especially their own. It was a cruel business from that perspective. People always wanted to feel they were in the know even when they didn't have a clue as to what the real truth was. When one station had juicy rumors, it would spread through the television and radio communities faster than a New York minute. The CBS Santa Barbara station family was the fodder for all the gossip right now. The truth didn't matter because it was about whoever had the best story to tell. That became everyone's truth at least until it was proven not to be true. Then it was just dismissed as if no one had ever brought it up in the first place.

David Pedderman had not really slept in twenty-four hours, except for the few minutes he got before the police woke him. He looked like he hadn't slept as he stumbled around the house occasionally picking up things off the floor and putting them back in drawers. The police were very good at going through stuff, but they didn't make any effort to put things away.

Pedderman had called Anna's cell phone at least a dozen times. He wanted to talk to her. She never picked up. He went into the garage and stood over the place where the police found the "hidden" plastic bag trying to figure out how that got there. Who put that in his garage and why would anyone do that? He even wondered if Anna didn't set him up herself. The mind plays a lot of funny games when you are sleep-deprived and under unmanageable stress. Pedderman had a lot of questions that he would never get answers to.

The ringing phone brought Pedderman back into the house. He had left his cell phone on the kitchen counter hoping that Anna would, at some point, return his calls. As he reached for the phone, he hoped it would be his wife; it wasn't.

"David, Stewart Simpson calling."

Pedderman recognized the voice even though he had only heard it a couple of dozen times over the past several years. Mr. Simpson had never called the sales manager before on his cell phone. Things were beyond surprising him anymore.

"Yes, Mr. Simpson, what can I do for you?"

"David, how are you holding up? I've been worried about you. Are you doing okay?"

"I'm doing as well as can be expected. I'm a little surprised by your phone call, sir."

"Look, you're one of our family and I'm concerned about you. You've done a good job year after year and I know how hard you've worked for my company. Is there anything I can do for you?"

Mr. Simpson sounds sincere, David thought.

Now Pedderman didn't know what to think. Was it possible that the owner of the station really did know what kind of job he had done for the CBS affiliate?

"Mr. Simpson, I really appreciate your call, but there isn't anything you can do for me unless you know a good attorney."

"Seriously, are you going to need one?"

"I don't think so, but I might. It doesn't appear that anyone believes me. I'm not even sure Lisa believes me." Pedderman was fighting back tears.

"David, I can help you. If you are truly innocent, then I want to help get your life back on track. Let's do this. I'm going to send Dugan, my assistant, to pick you up. Join me for dinner and you can fill me in on all the details and let's see if I can't help you out of this mess." Stewart was convincing.

"Mr. Simpson, you don't have to do this." Pedderman choked back a sob.

"I insist. You are part of our station family. Dugan is on his way. We'll have dinner and try to figure this out."

Over the next twenty minutes, Pedderman raced to get a hold of himself. A cold shower and a shave woke him up. Optimism seeped in. He wasn't quite sure what to wear to Mr. Simpson's house but he wanted to make a good impression. Maybe, just maybe, this could all go away. He could turn this around. Like most blatant liars, he could even lie to himself.

"Dugan, this is better this way. I don't want outside help, no matter how good they might be. The fewer people that are tied to this the better. We'll just keep this between the two of us. It's safer that way." Stewart told Dugan what he had expected to hear.

"It's the right call, boss. I'll go pick him up. I've got the rest of it handled." Dugan headed out the door to the car.

Twenty minutes later, Dugan arrived at the Pedderman house and went to the door to pick up the sales manager. Dugan was purposely not very talkative. Pedderman tried to start a conversation, but the owner's trusted assistant was not willing to open up, even the slightest.

Once the two arrived at the Home Ranch Estates, Dugan drove the car into the circular driveway, stopping at the entrance. Pedderman's eyes told the story that Dugan had seen so many times before from first-time visitors. As usual, Mr. Simpson greeted his visitor as Dugan opened the front door. David Pedderman was beginning to feel better and better about his situation. He truly felt like things might be changing for the better. *Maybe Mr. Simpson can really help, and maybe I can go back to work,* he thought.

Stewart Simpson was a master at making people comfortable, even though they might be out of their league around him. Pedderman was certainly out of his league with Mr. Simpson. Once Dugan was sure his boss and Pedderman were comfortable, he disappeared out the front door so he could bring the car around to the garage area. This was a familiar scene that had played out only weeks earlier when another station employee visited the home of the station owner.

"David, tell me, and I want you to be totally honest with me. I can't help you unless I know the truth." Stewart Simpson sounded as sincere as the Santa Barbara sky was blue. "Be totally honest. Did you kill Steve and Jesse?"

Pedderman put his head down, shaking it from side to side, and then he voiced what his head was saying, "No . . . no, no, no. I didn't kill anyone. I may be a lot of things, but I'm not a killer."

"What about the polygraph test? I heard it was inconclusive. Why do you think that was?"

"I don't know how to answer that, Mr. Simpson. I answered every question as honest as I could. I never killed anyone." The conversation was causing David Pedderman to get emotional again. He was a physical mess and no matter how hard he tried to hold it together in front of his owner, he wasn't doing a very good job. Simpson thought that was the only way a real innocent man would behave.

"Gentlemen, dinner is ready if you would follow me to the dining room." Dugan's interruption was right on cue. It was a welcomed change to a very tense conversation. As the three walked to the dining room, the house phone rang.

"Excuse me, please. I will answer the phone. Please be seated." Dugan left the room. A minute later he returned. "Mr. Simpson, it's a call you should take."

Stewart knew from Dugan's tone that the call was important. "Excuse me, David, I'll be right back."

"This is Stewart."

"Stewart, it's Lisa. Okay if I stop over this evening?" The question caught Stewart off guard. He planned this evening knowing that Lisa was not going to be available to him. "Lisa, it's not a good night. What about tomorrow night for dinner?"

That was not an answer Lisa was used to hearing. She wondered if Stewart was entertaining another lady friend. It bothered her that her jealousy kept creeping into her thoughts about the man she couldn't have on a full-time basis.

"I really need to see you tonight. Can I stop by later?"

Stewart could tell that Lisa wondered what he was doing. He didn't want any red flags, so he decided it was in everyone's best interest if he allowed her to stop by.

"Give me a few hours to finish up some work I'm doing. Why don't you come around nine?"

"I'll see you then. You won't be sorry. I really need you tonight."

Stewart hadn't heard Lisa express herself this way to him in a long time. She usually kept her passion protected from him. It excited him that she was voicing it, and combined with what he had planned for his guest, it was beginning to turn him on in a sick and twisted way. Stay in control, he told himself.

Entering the dining room where Dugan had already delivered the salads and poured the wine, Stewart took his seat across from Pedderman. "Sorry about that. David, have you talked to an attorney yet?"

"No. I didn't think I needed one, and quite honestly, I don't have any way to pay for an attorney. I really thought that once I took the polygraph that would clear me and I wouldn't be a suspect anymore."

"Look, the one thing you can't be, David, is naïve in this situation. This is a matter of your freedom and you're being looked at for two homicides. You need an attorney, and you needed one yesterday. I'm going to make a call, and tomorrow I'll set up a meeting for you." Stewart was trying to comfort Pedderman.

"Mr. Simpson, I can't tell you what that means to me. I feel like I'm in this all alone."

"What about your wife, David? How is she holding up?" Stewart's question hurt David to think about it.

Pedderman let his head hang down, as if he were in shame. "She left me."

"Do you think she thinks you killed these people?" the owner asked.

"No. I think she finally got tired of hearing all about my affairs. When she heard about my involvement with Jesse, that was pretty much the last straw."

Stewart noticed his guest wasn't eating. "David, please eat. You are going to need your strength. Dugan has prepared a great meal of steak and lobster. It's to die for." Little did Pedderman know how true that statement would be. That was Stewart Simpson's sick sense of humor. He thought of himself as a "Hannibal" persona, and even though his guest wouldn't get the severity of his humor, it was still fun in a sick way for Stewart to play this little game of words.

Stewart kept an eye on the clock. The one thing he didn't need was for Lisa to show up and find her sales manager at the house. He didn't want to give her anything else to make her more suspicious than she already was. He wasn't sure, but he did suspect that she wanted to come over this evening for more than just sex.

"David, tell me about your relationship with Jesse. How did the two of you hook up?" Stewart wanted to know the details because he didn't like the fact that someone was playing in his playground. When it came to the other sex, he was very much a kid in a candy store.

"I had an affair with her. That's all it was. I started to talk with her and knew she was upset about a relationship that she said went bad. I probably took advantage of her and we ended up together," Pedderman confessed. *I have to be honest if I want his help,* he thought.

Dugan, as usual, stayed close by to hear everything that was going on in the dining room. By this time he had picked up the salad plates and delivered the steak and lobster. He could tell by hearing his boss's voice and the questions he was asking that his boss was about to get agitated with his guest. Dugan knew how Stewart's ego and jealously worked when it came to women. His job now was to make sure that the rest of the evening went as planned. It was too late to make changes to tonight's master plan. The key was to keep the execution of the plan as in tact as possible to ensure its success. And to calm his boss down.

Dugan poured Pedderman another glass of wine. "How's your steak, Mr. Pedderman?"

"The entire menu is great. Thank you. It's been a long time since I've had steak and lobster." Turning to his host and speaking in a broken tone, "Mr. Simpson, thank you for inviting me this evening. You don't know what it means."

"David, we're going to get you through this. Have a little more wine," and with that Stewart poured into David's glass.

It was obvious to both Dugan and Mr. Simpson that their guest was starting to feel the effects of the sodium azide that was in the wine and the water. Pedderman was beginning to have trouble breathing. Sodium azide worked quickly shutting down the heart. Stewart had gotten up and gone to his library and returned to the table with a photo album. This was the meanness that Stewart displayed whenever he was going to crush his opponent. It wasn't good enough for him to just win, he wanted his opponent to know that he had destroyed him and controlled the entire situation from start to finish.

Pedderman was not innocent after all; he did have an affair. His whole life was an affair. But the only one that mattered was the one affair he had with Stewart Simpson's Jesse. In Stewart Simpson's mind, that justified making Pedderman the fall guy for everything.

Stewart opened up the photo album and put it in front of Pedderman. The color was beginning to go out of his face and his breathing became harder and harder. The sales manager knew as soon as he saw the first pictures that something was very wrong. There was Jesse with Stewart traveling in Europe, skiing in Switzerland, and playing around in Hawaii. Pedderman looked up at his host and it began to dawn on him that the whole night was a set-up. He started to think that this was what happened to Jesse and Steve, but he didn't know why. So he asked. Looking up at Stewart Simpson and Dugan, he simply said in a very quiet voice, "Why?" And with that his face fell to the table and he was dead.

21

DUGAN BROUGHT IN THE plastic tarp and laid it down on the floor. He got behind Pedderman's body, sliding the corpse onto the tarp. He then made sure every part of his body was wrapped and dragged him from the dining room to the kitchen where Stewart awaited with a plastic bag, similar to the one found in Pedderman's garage by the police. He took it and placed it in Dugan's trunk. Together the two men lifted the big sales manager and carefully placed him in the trunk. Dugan wasn't so sure how he was going to lift this big guy out of the trunk by himself. Stewart Simpson had to ready himself for Lisa, who would be arriving any minute.

"Are we clear on the plan? Are you sure you can handle the body by yourself?" Stewart asked his confidant.

"It's going to be tough, but what choice do we have?" Dugan had been there before, in fact, several times over the past twenty years.

"Get back here as quickly as possible. We don't want Lisa to question anything."

Dugan got in his car and drove out of the garage and headed the twenty minutes back to David Pedderman's house. He was hoping that Pedderman's wife was not going to have a second thought about coming home, at least not this particular night.

Stewart did his best to clean up the dishes and move everything off the table to the kitchen. This was not a job he ever did, so it was a struggle.

Dugan pulled into Pedderman's driveway. It was earlier than he planned, but he couldn't take a chance on Lisa discovering Pedderman at the house. It was not as dark as he wanted it to be, making the task trickier because he didn't have Pedderman's garage door opener. He got out of the car and quickly went to the front door where he let himself in with Pedderman's keys. He then closed all the blinds and opened the garage door. Pedderman's car was there but Anna's car was gone, so there was room for Dugan to pull into the garage and close the door.

Dugan mustered all his strength and began easing the body out of the trunk, keeping it wrapped in the plastic. He was very careful not to leave any DNA evidence behind anywhere. It took almost twenty minutes for Dugan to get the body out of the trunk, pull it into the house, and place the dead Pedderman at the dining table. Dugan then returned to the trunk and, taking the plastic bag that Stewart Simpson provided, took out the contents and left them next to the body—the gun and bullet found by the police. Dugan placed the revolver and bullet the police had found on the table. He then sat Pedderman's body in the dining room chair; he folded the arms on the table and leaned the corpse forward.

The final touch was a note that the police would find at some point that would appear to be a suicide note. Everything was in place.

Dugan backtracked, making sure to lock up the house and leave no traces. He then rushed home.

Lisa literally ended up following Dugan up the circular driveway. Stewart's assistant jumped out of his car to open Lisa's car door.

"Dugan, are you just getting back from a late-night run?" Lisa's question was simply innocent, but considering what Dugan had just done he wondered if she knew something.

"So, where's the ice cream?" she asked.

Dugan's expression told Lisa that he didn't have a clue what she meant by that. "Dugan, it's a joke. I thought maybe Stewart sent you out to the store or something," and after a couple of beats she added, "and the ice cream was just my wishful thinking."

"Oh, I wasn't quite sure what you were asking me." Trying to move off the conversation, Dugan quickly added, "Let me show you to the door. Stewart is anxiously waiting for you."

Nothing more was said as Lisa entered the big house. There, as if knowing she was coming through the door, was Stewart Simpson standing with his lover's glass of chardonnay. Stewart handed her the glass and gave her a slight embrace and Lisa responded unexpectedly by giving Stewart a very passionate kiss. Stewart hoped that sex would be her focus this night. He would love to lose himself with her physically. He didn't want to think about what had happened in his house before she arrived.

It was like time didn't exist for the next couple of hours. Stewart felt it as much as she did. Whatever was going on this evening, it was different for both of them. Different in a great way, and it wasn't just the sex. It was everything that two people who are passionately in love feel when things are right between the two of them.

Stewart knew he was in love with Lisa, but he had never let himself feel the way this night was feeling. He had always protected himself. Love was too complicated for him. In his mind, love was too expensive.

Few words were spoken over the hours they spent in Stewart's master bedroom. It was as if the two were making love for the first time and the last time, and both of them understood it. Stewart wasn't quite sure what to think about the emotions he was having. He wanted to hold Lisa and ask her what she was feeling. He wanted to know what was going on inside her, but he didn't want to chance getting an answer he couldn't handle. Instead, he just held her. He held her tight and so close their two hearts were beating together. It was the most intimacy the two had experienced in their entire life together, and neither knew what to do with these feelings.

As they lay together holding each other, Lisa broke the silence. "What if," she started and then stopped her words.

"What if," Stewart repeated as if to pry her next words from her lips.

"What if I were to leave Tom?" The embrace that was tightly holding the two together loosened as Stewart leaned away so he could look directly into his lover's eyes. He wanted to say the right thing. Instead he said nothing.

Lisa pulled Stewart closer and put her head under his chin as if she hadn't said anything. Stewart's lack of immediate response was his response. It had been that way for twenty years. Why did she think it would change now? As hard as Stewart struggled to say something, something that would let Lisa know how he truly felt about her, the words didn't come. And for the next fifteen minutes the two laid together embracing each other, neither one brave enough to express the love they both felt in fear of losing it all.

* * *

Dugan was in the kitchen finishing with the cleanup from dinner earlier that evening. Lisa entered fully dressed and ready to leave. "Do you have any coffee made?" Her voice was soft and quiet.

"Let me get you some." Dugan got out a cup and poured his guest a nice fresh cup. He knew she took a little milk, and without being asked, he prepared it exactly the way she liked it. Dugan was as much a part of this relationship as Stewart, only without the fringe benefits. He didn't quite understand why these two people had never made it a permanent thing. He was smart enough to know that was probably what kept the relationship alive.

"You know I love him," Lisa said looking directly at Dugan.

"And Mrs. Campbell, he loves you. More than he would ever admit," Dugan said as if he was saying it for Stewart.

Lisa didn't know if Dugan's reference to "Mrs. Campbell" was a reminder to her that she was the one married or if that was just his way of addressing her at this particular moment. "We've certainly been through a lot together, Dugan. Why have you stayed?"

Lisa's question was in search for an answer to her own question. Dugan and she were alike in many ways. They both endured a very long relationship with someone who probably wasn't capable of returning the same kind of relationship back to them, and yet they both stayed. She hoped Dugan would answer the question and that his answer might help explain her own staying power.

"Mrs. Campbell, I stayed because even with all his faults he stood beside me in my darkest moment. He gave me a place to come to terms with everything that was bad that I had to deal with." Dugan paused as he thought through his words. He didn't know how much Lisa knew about his relationship with Stewart. He assumed she knew more than anyone else outside of the three of them, but he still didn't know how much that was. "Lisa, he saved my life at one point."

"Was that when you lost your family?" Lisa said.

Dugan knew by her question that she knew more than he thought.

"Yes. That was a very dark moment for me and without Mr. Simpson I probably wouldn't be here talking to you right now." Dugan didn't want to be the center of the conversation anymore so he asked the only thing he could.

"What about you? Why have you stayed around all these years knowing it would never be more than a relationship of convenience?"

"I don't know. There were times I never wanted to see him again. But we have something that I can't explain. I love him, and truth be told, I love him more than my own husband." There. She had said it to someone else. "I better go." Lisa took a last sip from the cup and put it on the counter. She then walked over to Dugan and without hesitation leaned up and kissed him on his cheek. The two of them had something in common that gave them a bond few would understand. They shared Stewart Simpson and they shared deep, deep secrets. Secrets that only the two of them knew, and those were stories for another time.

22

"BARRY BURKE." THE NEWS DIRECTOR answered his cell phone while driving along the coast heading to work.

"Barry, its Richard. I wanted to give you a head's up that we're going to arrest David Pedderman sometime this morning. I'll call you when we are heading over there."

"Thanks, Richard. I'll have my people there."

Normally, the detectives never tipped the media about an arrest, but Richard Tracy and Skip Reynolds felt like the station was as much a part of this case as they were. They wanted to return the cooperation.

Barry pulled off the highway to make a call to the station. "John, get your cameraman and be ready to roll at any time this morning. I'll call you when it's time. The Santa Barbara police are going to arrest Pedderman sometime this morning. Be ready to go so you can capture it."

John's young reporter mind was running. He wanted to talk to Pedderman before the police arrested him. He knew all the reasons he shouldn't. He also knew the one reason he should; it is what good reporter's do.

John Rankin was impatient with his career. He knew he had

come a long way in a short time. He felt screwed when he tried to play by the system and rules of the news room when Carlos took the lead with the panhandling story. This rookie wasn't going to get beat again. Forget waiting for his photographer. He would go to the station, get the camera gear, and go alone. The only question in his mind was whether or not he should call Pedderman first or just show up. If he was going to do this, then he should just do it, he thought. *No phone call, no warning. I'll just show up and shoot my own interview. What's he going to do? The worst thing is he won't talk to me. No, the worst thing is he might hit me.*

John debated whether or not to tell Pedderman that the police were coming. *Get the interview first,* he thought. *See how that goes and then maybe tell him.*

The reporter pulled the car up in front of the Pedderman house. It looked dark, like no one was home. John sat for what seemed like an hour in his car talking himself through the scenario trying to build up his courage. Then he just said to himself, "Fuck it, let's do this." John got out of the car, opened the back door, and grabbed the camera gear.

Standing on the porch, the silence from inside the home was spooky. John knew Pedderman's wife had left and taken the kids. The silence was eerie. The reporter rang the doorbell once, then a second time, and then a third time. He couldn't really see into any windows. Surveying the neighborhood, he looked around to see if there was any activity on the street. There wasn't. It might have been the hour of the morning. Finally, he reached for the front door handle to see if the house was unlocked. It wasn't.

Debating his next move, he remembered Barry's story about how he and Detective Reynolds found Jesse's body. They got into the house through the back door, so reaching down to pick up his gear, he walked off the porch and around to the backyard gate. Luckily, there wasn't a lock on the gate, and he was able to reach his arm over and around to flip the latch. John was sure if any neighbors were watching, the police would probably be showing up really soon.

Drapes closed off all the windows. There was no way to get a view into the Pedderman home. John tried the back door leading out of the house from the patio slider. It was locked. Just by chance, and to make sure he had exhausted all his options, he walked over and turned the handle on the door leading to the backyard from the garage. It turned. John was in, at least in the garage. David's car was there. He touched the hood partly because he had seen that done a million times on those TV detective shows. The engine was cold.

Walking over to the door that led to the inside of the house, John's heart was beating faster than he ever remembered it beating before. The adrenaline was almost overwhelming. He kept reminding himself to stay calm, stay calm. The door leading to the kitchen was open. Now he was in.

As the reporter took his first step into the kitchen area he could see what looked to be David Pedderman slumped at the dining table with his face down in his folded arms as if taking a nap.

"David," John said quietly as if he didn't want to startle him. "David," this time his volume rose a couple of levels. There was no reaction.

John took a few steps closer, and with each step he sensed something was very wrong. Pedderman stayed in position and John noticed he wasn't moving, not even to take a breath. He wasn't breathing, and the young reporter almost collapsed from the realization that the sales manager was dead.

"Oh, fuck. Now what?"

At that moment his cell phone rang, almost giving him a heart attack.

"Hello." His voice trembled.

"John, its Barry." There was silence on the other end. "John, are you there?"

"Yes, this is John," he said almost in a whisper.

"Speak up. I can barely hear you. Are you ready to go? The police are heading to Pedderman's house right now. If you leave now you can get there in time to get shots of them taking him from the home to the police car. Talk to Richard Tracy. He told me he would give you a sound bite."

Barry expected some enthusiasm from the other end of the phone. What he got was more silence. John thought he had better get out of the house as fast as possible so the police wouldn't find him with a dead David Pedderman. It was too late.

Barry was still on the cell phone waiting to hear something from his reporter when there was a lot of noise and commotion coming through his cell phone. "John, John, are you okay?" Barry screamed into the phone.

No response. John stood frozen, trying to figure out his next move. The police had knocked on the door one time, announced themselves, and then broke in. Police with drawn guns entered the home. It wasn't SWAT, but to the young reporter it might as well have been. Detectives Tracy and Reynolds were next through the door. Imagine their surprise in seeing John Rankin, the young kid reporter from CBS, standing over David Pedderman.

The first policeman through the door immediately yelled to John to drop his weapon, not knowing it was a cell phone in his hand. John dropped it immediately and it hit the floor. John had seen enough TV and movies that he knew to follow orders before he got shot. Barry heard the commotion. "John, John, talk to me," came Barry's loud voice from the cell phone laying on the floor.

"Who's this on the line?" asked a familiar voice to Barry on the other end.

Barry recognized his police detective buddy's voice. "Richard, is that you? This is Barry. What the hell is going on?"

"We just got to the Pedderman home and when no one answered we broke the door down and found your reporter standing in the dining room."

"What? He was supposed to wait for my call. Where's Pedderman? Let me talk to John."

"Barry, slow down. You can't talk to John until we figure out what he is doing here. And if I'm not mistaken, it looks like Pedderman is dead."

"What? I'm coming over." Barry hung up the phone, threw on some pants and shoes and ran out the door. *What was going on? What was John doing in the Pedderman house? What was Pedderman doing dead? What the fuck and who the fuck killed Pedderman? And lastly: Come on Lisa, pick up the damn phone.*

"Hello?" It was a half-hearted attempt at answering her phone. It had been a long night. She began to wake up, recognizing her news director's voice on the other end. It didn't help that Stewart Simpson was gently groping her under the blankets.

"Barry, say that again," Lisa said.

"The police went to Pedderman's home this morning to arrest him. When they got there they found John Rankin, our rookie reporter, standing over Pedderman, who is dead. I don't know any more than that, but I'm heading over to the Pedderman house right now. I thought you might want to join me."

"Ok, I'm on my way." Lisa hung up the phone and got her naked body out from under the covers. Stewart didn't ask because he knew she would tell him what was going on. "I've got to run. The police went to Pedderman's house to arrest him and found our young reporter, John Rankin, there and Pedderman is dead. I don't know any more than that. I'll call you later today. Tom is gone another day so I'd like to see you again tonight."

"I'll let you know. I may have to fly back to Dallas. Call me when you get things under control and let me know what is going on." Stewart uncharacteristically got up from the bed and walked over to give Lisa a hug and a kiss goodbye.

A short time later, Lisa pulled her car on to the Pedderman street, but because of all the police action, including from the forensic team and the coroner's office, she had to park down the road. Walking up to the home, her thoughts were scattered about everything that had happened the past couple of months.

The police on the perimeter recognized Lisa Campbell and let her through the tape. Barry was inside the house talking to a handcuffed John Rankin, who was sitting on the couch. Barry saw his boss and walked over as she came through the front door. "Pedderman is dead. According to John, he came over to try and interview him before the police were going to arrest him."

"How'd he know the police were going to arrest him?" Lisa asked Barry.

"I told him. I was given a courtesy call about the pending arrest. I then called John and told him to be ready and that when the arrest was going down the police would tip us off. John thought it would be a good idea to try and interview David before he was taken in to custody. It's all a cluster. John showed up here and when no one answered the door he went around the back and got in from the garage door. He then finds Pedderman dead and that's when the police showed up."

"Did John have anything to do with his death?" Lisa felt she knew the answer already but had to ask the question.

"No." Barry and Lisa looked over at John sitting on the couch surrounded by an officer on each side. "The police are trying to just scare the shit out of him right now. They know he isn't guilty of anything but trying to move his career along. They'll release him after a while. Right now, they're just messing with him because I asked them to."

"What's the story with Pedderman?" Lisa asked.

"It appears it might be suicide. They found the same substance that they believe killed Steve and Jesse. You know, that chemical found in car airbags. They found a bunch of it when they did the original search on his house. He must have kept some extra around. They think he took it last night stressed with guilt. I think there was even a note."

"I would have never believed that he was capable of doing something like this. What do they think?" Lisa asked Barry.

"I've given up trying to figure out this case. Every time I think we have something it doesn't turn out to be close. Maybe he killed them because of jealously. Apparently he had a real thing for Jesse and after their little fling she rejected him and that apparently set him off. Steve was just in the wrong place at the wrong time. His death was more of a way to cover up the relationship between David and Jesse," Barry speculated.

Lisa couldn't believe what she was hearing. Thinking one step ahead of her competition, "Barry, you need to own this story and make sure our viewers know that we cover the worst, even if the worst belongs to some of our staff. Don't let anyone scoop you on your own story." Lisa's news prowess surprised Barry, and he was proud of her.

Barry knew that was how Lisa and he had always worked, but it was nice to have her say it. He immediately got on the phone to the newsroom and ordered up a live truck with Carlos as the lead reporter and a photographer. Using Carlos would piss John off, but that was the least of his worries. John was now part of the story.

***

Lisa walked away from everyone to a quieter part of the room. She dialed Stewart's home where Dugan answered. Within seconds Stewart was on the phone. "How bad is it?"

Stewart always wanted to know the bad news first.

"Pedderman is dead. John didn't have anything to do with it. It appears to be a suicide, and it looks as if Pedderman did the other two murders."

Silence was on the other end of the phone conversation. Stewart had signaled Dugan to pick up the extension when he got on the phone. The two men gave each other a thumb's up. So far, so good. "I'll be staying in Santa Barbara. I'll see you tonight." Stewart hung up the phone.

Lisa was happy with Stewart's last remark. She loved being cared for like a lover. "Lisa, Richard and Skip want to talk to us." Barry had walked over to get her so the four could meet in the kitchen where there was less of a crowd.

Reynolds took the lead. "It looks like a straight suicide. David left a note saying he killed Jesse because of a jilted affair. Then he had an opportunity to kill Steve trying to make Steve the bad guy, so it wouldn't draw any suspicion to him."

Barry wasn't buying how easy this all was. "This doesn't make any sense. Don't you think this is all too easy? It was like it was all tied up in a nice ribbon and handed to you. Doesn't that bother either of you?" Barry asked the detectives.

"Not really," Tracy said. "It means we've solved a double homicide and we get to clear it off our plate." Tracy had known his friend a long time and he knew how skeptical Barry could be. That was the nature of the news business.

"What about an autopsy?" Lisa's question fell on deaf ears so she asked it again. "Hey, what about an autopsy on the body?"

"There will be an autopsy, but this looks pretty open and shut. On another matter, how do you want us to handle the kid over there?" Tracy looked over at John still sitting in handcuffs on the couch.

"Is he in trouble?" Lisa asked.

"No. He was just stupid. We'll release him to you." Richard walked over to the couch and signaled one of the officers to stand the reporter up. He turned him around and unlocked the handcuffs. John didn't say a word. In his head he was just hoping not to get fired over this. Barry wasn't so sure that shouldn't happen.

Lisa, Barry, and John left the Pedderman house. Walking out the front door, John saw the CBS live truck with Carlos doing a special report from in front of the yellow crime tape. Once again he was beaten on his own story.

When the three arrived at the station, Barry told John to wait in his office. He walked with Lisa to her office. "What are you going to do with the kid?" Lisa asked.

"I'm thinking of letting him go. This is the second time he's done something stupid and missed his own story. He's got so much potential, but I'm not sure he will ever listen enough to be as good as he thinks he already is."

"Yeah, he reminds me of someone." Barry knew who Lisa was referring to. She didn't know Barry when he was starting out, but she had certainly heard all the stories. "You might think about your decision before you cut him loose. Finding good, new reporters is tough."

Barry didn't say anything but agreed with his boss. He didn't want to let the kid go and was hoping for some guidance from his GM. "What about this story, Lisa? How do you want us to play it?"

"We have to do the story and be above reproach. Cover it in great detail and don't leave anything out. Our viewers must know as well as the outside media that we won't pull any punches simply because it involves our own people."

"Tomorrow the coroner will do his preliminary autopsy. The police are asking for him to step up his toxicology reports. They want this thing wrapped up. I can't say that I blame them. What are you going to do with David's position? Anyone on the inside that can step up and fill the role as our new general sales manager?"

Lisa thought about the question. It was one she started thinking about before any of this current mess started happening. She had been unhappy with Pedderman's attitude and his feeling of being untouchable. "Linda is a good candidate, but I'm not sure if she's strong enough. The good news is that I don't have to decide that right now."

Barry left Lisa's office and headed back to John waiting in his office. John wasn't sure what was going to happen. He knew his decision to go to the Pedderman house was risky, but he felt it was still the right move. He would soon find out if his news director agreed with him.

23

LISA LEFT HER OFFICE and went to her house to check on things. She knew Tom would be calling to check in and she would want to fill him in on everything. He would probably hear about this on the news if he watched it that night. What she really wanted to do was to get refreshed and get over to Stewart's home. Lately her life had dealt with one crisis after another, and being with her boss, her lover, made things easier to handle.

On the drive to Stewart's, she listened to radio news stations. They were all over the death of David Pedderman. They were calling his death a suicide, and without any evidence to back it up, they blamed him for the earlier deaths of the two CBS news people. Local news didn't always have to confirm everything, especially when it had to do with a competitor they wanted to take down a peg or two. This story was a closed case for the news departments at the other television stations and radio stations. What else could have happened?

Dugan greeted Lisa's car as it pulled up the circular driveway. "It's so nice to see you this evening. Mr. Simpson is waiting for you." Dugan escorted Lisa from the car to inside the front door. As usual, Stewart was there with her glass of chardonnay.

The two had not talked since Lisa had left the house earlier that morning after getting the call about David Pedderman.

Stewart wanted to be filled in, especially since everyone in Santa Barbara was talking about their general sales manager being found dead. In Stewart's mind, it was if his involvement didn't register in his way of thinking. It was like he was hearing about Pedderman's death for the first time. Dugan, who had recognized this trait in his boss a long time ago, thought this was what made him so dangerous. Dugan was convinced that Stewart Simpson eliminated memories and thoughts of any wrongdoing from his mind as soon as the events were over. That's how his boss was able to sleep at night. This was something that didn't come so easy for Dugan.

Stewart led Lisa to their favorite place to talk. Lisa sat on the couch with Stewart sitting across from her on the foot stool within an arm's length from her. He loved looking into her eyes and being able to rub her legs while he listened to her talk.

"Fill me in on your sales manager's death. What happened?"

"Stewart, this is the weirdest thing I've ever been through. First my main anchor, then an intern, and now my general sales manager. I'm not sure what to think about it." Lisa paused to compose herself. The events of the day had finally caught up to her and she was beginning to get emotional, which was something she avoided all day. "The police believe it's now a closed case. They believe Pedderman killed Jesse for some jealously issues and then he killed Steve in order to divert any attention off himself. Their theory is that Pedderman then killed himself full of guilt and knowing the police were on to him."

"Were the police on to him?" Stewart asked.

"I think the police were on to him. We know when they showed up at his house they were there to arrest him for the murders," Lisa said.

"Well, there you have it. It sounds as if they were not only on to him but that they probably had the evidence to back it all up."

"The good news is that all this should be confirmed after the autopsy is done tomorrow. That should provide the DA's office with everything they need to close the case." Lisa leaned her head on the back of the couch and took a drink of wine. She had gotten quiet. Stewart knew this silence and prompted her to tell him what she was thinking. She didn't know if she should be honest with him or just act as if nothing was on her mind.

Saying nothing was always safer, but tonight she wanted to have the conversation.

“Stewart, there was a point over the past couple of weeks that I thought you might be involved in these deaths. I don’t know why, but it is what I thought about at times. I’m sorry. I’m sorry I ever thought that about you.”

“I know. Don’t worry about it. Let me ask you though, why would you ever think such a thing?” Stewart asked.

Lisa didn’t hesitate. “I think it was more jealously on my part than anything else. When I heard that you were involved in getting Jesse her job at the station my mind just ran from there. Then I realized that you were just helping a stranger because someone asked you to.”

Stewart wondered if Lisa had said anything to her detective friends. He wondered it but didn’t verbalize it. Dugan stood where he always did so he could hear as much of the conversation as possible. He also wondered if Lisa had said anything more to the police about Stewart’s relationship. If she had, the police would have investigated more than what they did. He was sure of this.

“Lisa, what happened to these three people was a tragedy and we may never know what went on in David Pedderman’s mind that caused him to commit these terrible murders. The bottom line is that we may never know.”

Lisa nodded her head in agreement. Dugan entered the room and called for dinner to be served. The pair got off their seats and headed for the dining room. Dugan refilled Lisa’s glass with the chardonnay she loved. Her mind kept returning to an easier time, the time when she first met Stewart Simpson twenty years ago.

Dugan looked at Stewart several times, waiting to see if he would give him the same sign he did last night when the sales manager had dined at the house. The sign was a confirmation to Dugan that they needed to follow through with their plan. The two had never discussed a plan to deal with Lisa, but Dugan was beginning to think that maybe they should have. Her suspicion and the little things that she had picked up over the many, many years made her a threat. Dugan was the sensible one and he certainly wasn’t thinking with his cock. That couldn’t always be said about Stewart. In fairness to Stewart, he was well beyond the sexual reasons for keeping Lisa around. Lisa was more than sex and Dugan knew that as well. He just didn't like loose ends, especially when it involved the threat of their freedom. This was something that Stewart Simpson had taught him very well.

Dinner was an event tonight and not something to rush through. Stewart did everything he could to make Lisa feel better about her day. He knew she had been through a very rough time. Two more glasses of wine and two hours later she was ready for bed. And tonight, she would sleep.

***

The morning was well underway when Lisa's cell phone went off. It was Barry calling. "Lisa, I'm at the coroner's office and guess what?"

Lisa was still trying to wake up. "What?"

"The medical examiner found traces of the drug sodium azide in Pedderman, the same drug that killed Steve and Jesse."

"What's the big deal about that? Everyone already thought that was how he killed himself."

"I know that. Here's the kicker. The coroner found steak and lobster in his stomach. It seems to be the dinner of choice. Every one of these three people had steak and lobster as their last meal." Lisa realized Barry was right. Every one of the victims, her employees, had steak and lobster in their stomach when they turned up dead.

Lisa's thoughts started taking her out of the conversation. She remembered Dugan cleaning up the kitchen the other night when she came over. It got her attention because it appeared that there were enough dishes for three and she saw lobster claws with the scraps of food. That would have been David Pedderman's last night alive.

"Lisa, are you still there?" The voice on the phone brought her back to reality.

"Sorry, I was distracted for a minute. Let me know if the coroner comes up with anything else." Flipping the cell phone closed, her mind started putting together the little bits of information she had picked up on over the past several weeks. *Is it possible that Stewart's involved?* Lisa had that reoccurring thought several times during this ordeal, but she always discounted it. Now she wondered if she should confront Stewart with her suspicions. Or could that put her life in jeopardy? *No, there's no way he'd ever hurt me,* she thought. *Then again, if he was capable of murder, then maybe I don't know him very well at all.*

Lisa asked herself what part Dugan might have played. "He would have had known. No, there is no way these thoughts have any bearing to the truth." Lisa caught herself saying these words out loud as Stewart walked into the room.

"What are you mumbling to yourself about?" he asked.

"Oh, nothing." She was startled to find Stewart standing there. She wanted to ask him. She wanted to tell him everything she was thinking. She just didn't know if she could trust her instincts. She wanted to trust that he wouldn't do anything to hurt her if she was uncovering the real truth.

"Dugan has prepared breakfast for us on the patio. Shall we?" Stewart held out his hand to the lady he had spent the past twenty years with. What would she think if she knew the truth about him all these years? What would she think if she knew his involvement with Steve, Jesse, and now David? Stewart's whole life was a mystery to those not only on the outside but on the inside as well, and that was how he liked it. *The price of wealth,* she thought.

The two walked hand in hand through the house to the outside patio area. It was a beautiful day in Santa Barbara and the sun was warming. For a moment, Lisa's thoughts about Stewart disappeared as she let the sun hit her face.

***

Sitting in the sun drinking hermosas made the real world seem a thousand miles away. Dugan had prepared a small feast of soft boiled eggs, salmon, bagels, and some very fresh fruit. The Sunday paper was on the table but neither Stewart nor Lisa picked it up. The two seemed to be lost in their own thoughts until Stewart broke the silence.

"Do you know what today is?" It was a happy question and she noticed he was smiling when he asked it.

Lisa thought for several moments but nothing registered. "I'm afraid I don't," she replied.

"Well, think back. Think back twenty plus years. Today was the date we first made love." Stewart seemed very proud of remembering this date. Lisa and Stewart never seemed to recognize any specific anniversaries or dates that might actually mean something to most couples. But then again, they weren't your traditional couple.

"Oh, my god, how did you remember that particular date?" Lisa was impressed. She wondered if Stewart had just made up the date knowing she wouldn't know if it was accurate or not. It didn't matter because right now she believed him, and it made the morning very special to her.

"I remember all our important dates."

Over the next several minutes, Stewart rattled off some key dates that had occurred over the years of sharing so much intimate time together. Lisa was in tears by the time Stewart had finished. It dawned on her that Stewart had the same feelings for her as perhaps she had for him. Today her tears were happy tears.

Stewart reached over with his left hand and wiped the tear drops that began to run down her cheek. As he did this, his right hand came up to the table and put down the box every woman recognizes from Tiffany's. This was very out of character for Stewart. He never gave her jewelry because he was sensitive about Tom's feelings and didn't want to put it in his face. Lisa could hardly contain herself when she saw the turquoise box.

"What is it?" she questioned as if knowing Stewart wouldn't tell her.

"Open it. I wanted to give you something very special to commemorate our time together. I've never told you what you mean to me and I wanted to do this for you."

Lisa's hands couldn't move fast enough as she removed the ribbon to open the box. *Earrings or a ring, or maybe a very expensive brooch?* Whatever it was it didn't matter, and explaining anything to her husband, Tom, was the furthest thing from her mind right now.

She carefully opened the box to find a gold key. It was on a Tiffany key ring inscribed, *To My One Love, Lisa.*

"Stewart, what did you do?" Lisa looked at Stewart with a deep love.

"I got you something special. The key fits a new Maybach

that is sitting in the driveway waiting for you." He reached over and touched her hand. She was in shock and couldn't believe Stewart's generous show of love and affection. He was always generous, but this was different. His emotions were different and even his words were different.

"Twenty years is a long time. We've had some great moments and you are the one true love of my life. I want you to know that." Stewart was talking from his heart maybe for the first time in his life.

Lisa was overwhelmed and stood up from the table to hug her lover. The two then walked through the house to the front entry and out to the circular driveway. There with a huge bow on top was her new, $400,000 blue with black trim Maybach. She had never seen such beauty before in a car. Then she noticed the license plate read, "20YEARS." For a brief moment she thought, *Perfect, this is how I explain this to Tom.* Lisa knew that Stewart had already thought of that.

"Stewart, it is fabulous." She walked around it as if to notice every little detail. She sat in the driver's seat and laughed. She looked at Stewart and knew this man, this generous, lovely man was everything she thought he was. Amazing, strong, smart, and the love of her life. Not in the least involved in any crime. Ever.

The two returned to their patio table. They were both very content sitting in the sun and daydreaming in their two very different worlds. Lisa thought back twenty years ago to that time when she first met Stewart Simpson. She had started her broadcast career as a reporter at the ABC station in Palm Springs, California.

The memories flooded her head as she remembered what seemed like every detail. No one would believe the life she lived.

Dugan refreshed the hermosas and then quietly disappeared, much like he entered the room. It was his job to take care of every single detail for Stewart Simpson. A job he did incredibly well and was paid handsomely for. He knew that he was paid for his silence as well. That didn't keep him from writing in his daily diary. That was his insurance; a nuclear bomb that could destroy his boss, himself, and probably a few very important businessmen and politicians in the country. For now, and probably forever, Dugan would keep those journals a secret, allowing his boss to kill again.